Azalea,
Unschooled

Other Middle Reader and Young Adult books by Islandport Press

Cooper and Packrat: Mystery on Pine Lake
Cooper and Packrat: Mystery of the Eagle's Nest
by Tamra Wight

Lies in the Dust:
A Tale of Remorse from the Salem Witch Trials
by Jakob Crane and Timothy Decker

Billy Boy:
The Sunday Soldier of the 17th Maine
by Jean Mary Flahive

Uncertain Glory
by Lea Wait

The Fog of Forgetting
by G. A. Morgan

Mercy: The Last New England Vampire
by Sarah L. Thomson

Azalea,
Unschooled

by Liza Kleinman
illustrated by Brook Gideon

ISLANDPORT PRESS

ISLANDPORT PRESS
PO Box 10
Yarmouth, Maine 04096
www.islandportpress.com
books@islandportpress.com

Copyright © 2015 by Liza Keierleber
Illustrations copyright © 2015 by Brook Gideon
First Islandport Press edition published May 2015

All Rights Reserved

ISBN: 978-1-939017-58-1
Library of Congress Control Number: 2014911180

Book jacket design: Karen Hoots/Hoots Design
Book design: Michelle Lunt/Islandport Press

To Anya

Chapter 1
Unschool Meeting

The first time I met Gabby, she was in a big mollusk phase and had baked some experimental snail cookies.

"Try one," she urged, holding out a plate.

I didn't even know her name yet. I had just moved to Maine, and was standing in a stranger's living room at a party for home-schoolers. Every place we'd lived—and there had been a lot of them—my mother had always made sure we met other home-schoolers. She said it was important to be part of a community.

Gabby, still offering me the plate, took a cookie for herself and had a large bite.

"They're delicious," she said encouragingly.

The cookies were lumpy and swollen, and each one had two thin pieces of black licorice sticking out. I weighed my love of cookies against my lukewarm feelings toward snails.

"Are those supposed to be antennas?" I asked, stalling for time.

"Tentacles," she explained, chewing. "Mollusks have tentacles."

Then she laughed, covering her mouth just after the crumbs sprayed onto me. She had golden-brown hair, thick and curly, that was the exact same color as her skin and her eyes. Everything about her was golden-brown.

"You didn't think the cookies had actual snails in them, did you?" she asked.

I gave her a nervous smile.

"No," I lied.

"They're just *shaped* like snails," Gabby said kindly, brushing the crumbs from my shoulder. "I should have explained that."

She examined the remains of the cookie in her hand.

"I guess they're not even so snail-shaped, after all. They looked swirlier before I baked them."

I took a cookie and had a bite. Chewing gave me an excuse to look around for a while before I had to talk again.

The room was enormous—it was the biggest living room I'd ever seen. Giant paper words hung from the ceiling: EXPLORE. CRE-ATE. QUESTION. WONDER. DO. I'd never been to a party that provided so many directions. Was I supposed to do all of these things at once, while eating snail cookies, or could I tackle the list one at a time?

There were a lot of adults in the room, wandering around and talking to each other, but only a few kids. My mother was having a conversation with another parent, and my sister Zenith sat slumped in a chair near the food table. She looked annoyed. She was thirteen, two years older than me, and she almost always looked annoyed.

I swallowed my piece of cookie and was about to ask Gabby if she knew most of the people here when a woman climbed up onto a chair. She had greeted us when we'd arrived at the party. It must be her house, I figured, especially since she was allowed to stand on the chairs. She began tapping a spoon against a glass for attention, even though everyone was already looking at her.

"Hello, hello!" the woman shouted, still tapping. Her gray-blonde hair tumbled wildly, and with her spoon-holding hand she gave a little wave that almost threw her off balance. The buzz of conversation died down.

"I'm so glad to see all of you here today," the woman said. "For those of you who are seasoned unschoolers, thank you so much for coming to share your experience. And I want to give a warm welcome to those of you who are homeschoolers, or even, dare I say"—the woman lowered her voice and delivered the end of her sentence with a dramatic quaver—"*schoolers.*" There was laughter.

"That's my mom," whispered Gabby.

So she lived here, in this beautiful old house filled with furniture that looked like someone had carved it. My family had just moved into an apartment. It was nice enough, but I had been hoping for a yard. This house, I had noticed when we arrived, had lots of land around it.

"That's nice that your mom organizes meetings for homeschoolers," I said, whispering now, since all attention was on the host. "We just moved here. My mom is always looking for other homeschoolers for us to get together with. I guess that's how she found out about this party."

Gabby looked at me in surprise.

"*Un*schoolers," she said, a little too loudly. "This meeting is about *un*schooling."

Before I could ask what the difference was, Gabby's mother continued speaking. She still held the spoon and the glass, but she had stopped tapping them together.

"Let me introduce myself," she said. "For those of you who don't know me, I'm Spirit, and I want to thank you all for coming here today with open minds and adventurous hearts."

"*Spirit?*" I whispered, not very politely.

"She's calling herself that now," Gabby whispered back. "Her real name is Muriel."

Spirit continued.

"For us, unschooling has been a wonderful journey, and we're so excited to have your company. I know that some of you here are homeschooling, and I'd like to congratulate you on taking the first step away from an outdated, stifling idea of childhood." Spirit paused, beaming.

There was a stir of activity in the room as the parents looked around at each other, trying to figure out whether to be proud or insulted. I wondered if Mom would be annoyed that this had turned out not to be a homeschoolers' meeting at all. She probably wouldn't care too much. She would just as soon be at a meeting, any meeting, than home unpacking with Dad. She liked meetings; she didn't care for unpacking. Still, I had been hoping to come back to this house, to play in the large yard with this new girl. I hoped that wasn't ruined now.

"I'm Gabby," she said softly, holding out her hand.

I took her hand and shook it. I had never actually shaken someone's hand before. It seemed like something adults did, maybe at important business meetings.

"I'm Azalea," I replied.

"Pretty name!" said Gabby.

"Thanks. It's a kind of flower. My sister's name is Zenith. It means highest point."

"That's an interesting name."

"The funny thing," I told her, "is that it used to be a brand of TV. A long time ago. Sometimes when Zenith is being particularly boring, I'll hold my hand toward her like a remote and pretend to change channels."

Gabby giggled. "That's funny." She paused. "I wish I had an interesting name. But I came with the name Gabby, so my mother kept it."

I wasn't sure what that meant. I hoped Gabby would explain, but she didn't.

Spirit continued speaking.

"I'd like to encourage you all to join us in taking the next step. As homeschoolers, you understand the value of letting your children learn at a pace and in a manner that suits them. Why, then, should you cling to the last shred of the old model—the one in which the deciding figure is the teacher, or, in this case, the parent? Why not give each child the freedom to discover his or her own truth?"

Gabby looked like she'd heard all of this before.

She also seemed unsurprised when a tall, skinny girl dressed entirely in pink ran up and grabbed her.

"Gabs!" the girl shrieked. She didn't appear to care that Gabby's mother was still talking. She surrounded Gabby in a hug, smothering her with her pink-sweatered arms. Even her jeans were pink.

"Hi," said Gabby, hugging back, still keeping her voice low. She pointed at me. "This is my new friend, Azalea."

I felt pleased. Already I was Gabby's friend! I was pretty sure Zenith hadn't made a friend yet. She was still slumped in her chair, gazing across the room at a chubby blond teenage boy who wasn't gazing back.

"Azalea, this is my friend Nola. She unschools, too. We do a lot of stuff together, projects and things."

Nola gave me a hard look. "Are you going to unschool?" she asked.

"I homeschool," I explained. "I think my mother thought this was a homeschoolers' meeting."

"Too bad," said Nola coolly, then turned back to Gabby.

"Gabs, come with me. I have stuff to tell you."

"Nola," Gabby said, "Azalea just moved here. She's new in town."

"I heard," Nola replied. She looked at me again. She studied my face, and I got the uneasy feeling that she knew something about me.

"Come *on*." Nola grabbed Gabby by the arm and yanked her off into another room.

Gabby turned toward me as they left, and called softly, "Talk to you later!"

I lifted a hand in a wave.

Spirit wound up her speech and commanded everyone to mingle. Now that Gabby was gone, I didn't know who to talk to. I moved toward Zenith's chair and stood next to it. Zenith did not acknowledge me. She chewed absently on a chunk of bread dipped in green-flecked hummus.

"I met the girl whose mom was speaking," I told her.

Zenith nodded. She was still looking across the room at the boy, whose head bobbed rhythmically between a pair of earbuds.

"Do you know who that is?" she asked, jutting her chin toward him.

"No," I said. "I don't know who anyone is except that lady and her daughter and the daughter's annoying friend."

"That's three more than me," Zenith pointed out. She ran a hand through her long, straight dark hair. I had always envied Zenith's hair. It was far more interesting and dramatic than mine, which was light brown and sort of cloud-shaped.

7

I spotted Gabby across the room, near where Spirit had been talking. Nola seemed to have disappeared, which was good. I went to talk to Gabby again, and Spirit rushed up, her long skirt rustling, her jungle of hair floating behind her. She ignored me.

"Gabby," she said, "where's your brother? We need chairs."

Gabby pointed to the boy wearing the earbuds.

"Gibran!" shouted Spirit. Everyone at the party turned except for Gibran. "Go get chairs from the garage!"

Gibran remained seated.

"And off he hustles," said Gabby, "breaking all records for speed!"

Suddenly Zenith appeared next to him. "I'll help you," she offered.

Gibran looked irritated, but he eased himself from between the earbuds and walked to the door. Zenith followed. I could hear her chattering at his back as they left. When they came back they were lugging folding chairs.

"Right here," directed Spirit, who was at once chatting with guests, ladling mugs of squash soup, and arranging furniture. No one sat in the chairs, but Spirit seemed satisfied, and whirled off to another part of the room.

I pointed to one of the signs hanging overhead.

"Did you make these?" I asked.

"No," Gabby replied. "That's a Spirit thing. I'm just the cookie maker."

This reminded me that I'd left the rest of my snail cookie on the plate, which was now across the room from us. I didn't feel like winding through the sea of people to find it.

"So, you live *here*?" I asked Gabby. I tried to imagine having a house like this. I could live on a whole different floor from Zenith, instead of sharing a room with her.

"Yes," she said. "All my life, just about. How about you—
have you ever been to Maine before? "

"No, not until we moved to Portland last week," I said. "My
dad is going to drive a tour bus."

Now that I'd said it aloud, it sounded strange. Who drove a
tour bus in a city that was completely new to him? Dad did. It
only sounded strange if you didn't know him.

Gabby didn't appear to notice. "So where did you live
before?"

"Oh, different places . . ."

I wasn't sure how it would sound to her, the way we had
moved around. I could barely remember all of the places we'd
lived. The earliest I could remember was Philadelphia, where my
parents had run a sort of clothing boutique for pets. Dog hats,
cat pants—if it would embarrass a pet, they carried it. That
hadn't lasted long. Then they'd owned a sewing supplies store in
Florida, called Darn It All, followed by an all-you-can-eat breakfast buffet in North Carolina. I could still remember the sicken-
ing smell of scrambled eggs in big metal bins. Most recently, they
had taken a stab at running an apple orchard in Connecticut. It
might have worked out, my father thought, if not for a late
frost.

"Well, I'm glad you're here now," said Gabby.

"Me, too," I said, and I meant it.

We watched Gabby's brother and Zenith, who was still talking, even though Gabby's brother was listening to his music
again. She hadn't said that much to me in the past year.

"So that's your brother?" I asked Gabby.

"Yeah," Gabby said. "He's fifteen."

"Does he unschool, too?" I asked.

"He does," said Gabby. "But I don't think he's that good at it. He mostly just sits around. He is building a boat, though."

"He doesn't look like you," I said.

Gabby didn't look quite like anyone I had ever seen.

"Gibran is Spirit's biological son," Gabby explained. "I'm adopted."

"Oh," I said.

I'd known plenty of other families with adopted kids; why hadn't I figured it out?

"How about you and Zenith?" Gabby asked.

"We're both"—I remembered Gabby's word—"biological. Although sometimes I think Zenith came from another planet."

We laughed.

"Sometimes I think I did," said Gabby, but she wasn't laughing anymore. She looked a little dreamy.

"Planet of the Snails?" I asked.

This made Gabby laugh again.

"Yes," she said. "My birth mother was a squid. They're mollusks, too, you know, like snails are. Huge ones."

"Wow," I responded. "I didn't know you were a secret squid!"

"Maybe you are, too," Gabby said. "Maybe we're Secret Squid Sisters!"

Nola appeared behind Gabby just as she said this. I had hoped she'd left.

"Me, too!" Nola shouted. A couple of people turned to look. Nola didn't care. She seemed more like Spirit's daughter than Gabby did.

"I want to be a Squid Sister, too!" Nola said, grabbing Gabby's hands and dancing in a circle with her, like that was some kind of a squid thing. For all I knew, maybe it was. Maybe unschoolers were the world's leading experts on squid. Personally, I was more interested in history, but to each her own.

Gabby pulled one hand from Nola's and held it out to me, but Nola yanked the hand back and turned away to make it clear the dance did not include me.

Message received, I thought.

Chapter 2

Unschool Bus

"So," Mom asked Zenith and me on the way home, "what did you think of the party?"

"Boring," said Zenith, not unpredictably. She was riding in the passenger seat next to Mom.

"Fun," I corrected from the backseat. "Good food. And I really liked that girl, Gabby, the one whose mom did the talking."

"I saw you talking to Nola, too," Mom said. "The girl dressed all in pink. Do you know who she is?"

Sure, I thought. *Gabby's obnoxious friend who hates me.*

"That's Jack's niece. You know, Jack—the old friend of Dad's who sold him the tour bus. The guy who moved to Florida. That's how I heard about the meeting today. He knows that we homeschool, and he got me in touch with some people."

So Nola's family was responsible for our owning the bus *and* for our being at the meeting. I remembered the way she'd looked at me when Gabby introduced us. She had known something about me, after all. Gabby probably knew, too. I was the only one who had been kept in the dark. Zenith, too, but she probably wouldn't care.

"The meeting," Zenith broke in, "was about *un*schooling, whatever that is. Why did we even go? I thought it was going to be a homeschooling thing."

"I think the idea of unschooling is kind of interesting," Mom said carefully. She held up a finger—*Give me a minute*—while she studied a street sign and then squinted at a sheet of paper with printed directions. "I think it's this way," she said, turning the car. "Anyway, it's a whole different philosophy. Unschooling. It's really about not imposing a structure on the natural curiosity of a child. I've been doing some reading about it."

"I see," said Zenith. "The last time you were doing some reading about something we ended up eating oatmeal and kale at every meal for a month."

I remembered this well. Zenith was exaggerating, but not by much.

"It was not every meal," Mom pointed out, switching lanes. "It was two out of the three, and if we'd stuck with it, we all would've lived to be a hundred and seven."

"Not worth it," said Zenith.

"Definitely not," I agreed.

We rode in silence for a while until Zenith spoke again.

"So kids who unschool don't have to do anything all day? Like, they could just lie in the middle of the floor all day if they wanted to?"

"Is that what you would do, Zenith?" Mom glanced over at her.

"Maybe. Probably not."

"I would," I said, partly to punish Mom for not telling us in advance about Nola's uncle, and partly because maybe it was true. "I'd just lie there and look at the ceiling and think about stuff."

"Maybe you would for a while," Mom suggested, "but I think that sooner or later you would think of something better to do."

"Anyway," Zenith said, "it doesn't matter. We're home-schoolers. If Azalea and I tried to lie on the floor all day, you'd be standing over us, waving your activity log and your list of goals. You'd drop kale on our heads until we got up."

"Actually," Mom said, "I was thinking we might give it a try."

"Dropping kale on our heads?" I asked. I tried to picture the wrinkly green leaves, dropping like rain.

"Unschooling."

At first, I thought I must have misheard.

"You want *us* to try unschooling? The thing where there's no teacher, no plans, nothing?"

Mom slowed to read a street sign, and swung the car into a U-turn.

"I think it could be a very valuable step. You girls are both smart, curious, capable people. Maybe it's time I stopped imposing my ideas of what you should know and do."

Zenith turned to face the backseat, and we exchanged a look. I knew she was thinking the same thing I was—that it would be great to decide, all by ourselves, what to do all day. It would also be a little scary. We were used to those lists of goals and activities. Like oatmeal and kale, they were good for us.

"Don't think you would be completely on your own," Mom said. She stopped for a moment to consult her directions before making a right turn. "I'll still be here to help you if you want it. But you'll be in charge of your journey, not me."

She noticed a stop sign and slammed on the brakes. Everyone jerked forward, and Zenith said, "That's probably a good thing."

Mom ignored that and guided the car to a stop in front of our building. I hadn't even realized we were back on our street.

Our apartment was in a narrow, three-story house, just like all the others on the block. It was close to the bay, and I could smell salt water when we got out of the car. Though it was the end of April, the air felt damp and chilly. The trees were still mostly bare. In Connecticut, everything had been green already.

Mom dug through her pocketbook for her key and let us into the apartment.

We lived on the first floor of the house. I had hoped there would be kids on the other two floors, but there weren't. On the second floor there was a young man and woman who walked their cat outside on a leash. They would have been perfect customers for my parents' pet boutique. On the third floor lived two older women who went everywhere on bicycles.

Zenith and I had bicycles, too, but I hadn't used mine yet. I pretended to myself that it was because I was too busy, but really it was because I was afraid to ride around in a strange city.

Zenith was not. She had already gone by herself for long rides, not even asking me if I wanted to come. Sometimes she stayed out so long that I knew she had gotten lost, though she would never admit it. Mom and Dad didn't mind, as long as she was back before dark. Mom said that she trusted us to know our boundaries and make good decisions.

"So what do you girls think?" Mom asked, pulling off her jacket. "Do you want to give unschooling a try?"

"I think it would be great," I told her. "I can unschool with Gabby. She knows all about how to do it right."

"There's no right or wrong," Mom reminded me. "That's part of what makes it so different."

She turned toward Zenith, who was preparing to vanish into the bedroom that we shared.

"What about you?"

Zenith paused, halfway through the door.

"I guess so," she said. "I'm willing to try it." Then she was gone.

Mom looked relieved. "Then it's settled," she told me. "We'll try it and see how it goes."

I walked into the kitchen and sat down at the table. My father was already there, a map spread out in front of him. He did not look up.

"Did you hear the news?" I asked. I never got to be the one with a breaking story. Usually Zenith whipped in ahead of me.

"What news?"

"We're not homeschooling anymore."

He looked up. "So you and Zenith have decided to give unschooling a try?"

I slumped down in an exaggerated show of disappointment. "You knew about this?"

"Your mother and I do talk sometimes, you know," Dad said.

I sighed. There was no point trying to surprise anyone in this house. I changed the subject.

"How is the bus business going?"

"Ask me in a few weeks," he said.

Dad planned to start the tours sometime in May, when spring would arrive in full force, along with out-of-state visitors. Before we'd left Connecticut, he had explained to us that lots of people came to visit Portland when the weather got warm. They wanted to get away from the hot places where they lived, and feel the cool ocean breezes in Maine. They would pay good money to be driven around the city and shown the sights.

By someone who knows what the sights are, Zenith had added pointedly.

Now, Dad slid his chair back from the table.

"How would you like to come along tomorrow for a test ride?" he asked.

"You mean it?" I asked.

None of us had seen the bus yet except for Dad. It was kept in a garage at the outskirts of the city. Two months before we'd moved here, Dad's friend had called to offer him the bus. Dad had driven up to look at it. He ended up buying it and signing the papers to rent an apartment. Then he'd driven back to Connecticut and told us to start packing.

"Sure," he said. "It's almost spring. If I'm going to be ready for those tourists, I'd better start learning my way around the city."

The next morning I was dressed and ready early. Dad pointed toward Zenith's and my bedroom door.

"See if your sister wants to come."

If Zenith came along, she would just be sulky and ruin everything. Still, I knocked on the door and went in. Zenith was lying on her bed, staring at the ceiling.

"Looks like you're already unschooling," I told her, which made Zenith smile a little through her scowl. "Listen, Dad is going to take the tour bus for a practice run. You want to come? We can ride in it and everything."

Zenith continued to study the ceiling. "It's like taking a little sail on the *Titanic* before it sets out for the open seas."

"What's that supposed to mean?" I asked.

We had studied the *Titanic* the year before, part of a unit Mom had thought up. The *Titanic* was an enormous ship that had sunk after hitting an iceberg. We also studied the *Hindenburg*, a gigantic airship that had blown up right while it was landing. Zenith said that in Mom's mind, the unit was called "Great Disasters and How They Could Have Been Avoided with a Little More Planning."

"I think you know what it means," Zenith replied quietly. She turned onto her side to look at me. "It means that this business of his has the same chance of success as his orchard, or his breakfast buffet, or his cat pants store."

"You have to have a little faith in things," I scolded.

"*I* have to have faith in things? I'm not the one who decided to abandon the orchard because of one bad year. I'm not the one whose motto is, 'If at first you don't succeed, move the whole family to a new city so you can try a brand-new half-baked scheme.' "

I needed to defend Dad.

"Giving tours is a good business. People pay lots of money."

"If it's such a great business," Zenith asked, "why did his friend unload it for cheap?"

I shrugged. "He probably retired. Mom did say he moved to Florida."

Zenith resumed her study of the ceiling. "Probably. He probably took his millions and moved someplace hot and sunny to enjoy his wealth, and out of the kindness of his heart, he's giving Dad a crack at the good life."

I started for the door. It was best not to deal with Zenith when she was in one of these moods. "So do you want to come or not?"

"Not," said Zenith, and I closed the door firmly—not a slam, exactly—behind me.

Dad grabbed the set of bus keys off his dresser. I scooped his map of the city from the kitchen table. He had outlined the path from our house to the garage with a yellow highlighter. In red pen he had traced the route he was planning for the tour.

"Don't forget this," I said.

Dad tucked it under his arm, and we were off.

While we drove out to the garage, I asked him about the tours.

"How will you know what to say?" I asked. "Do you know stuff about the sights around here?"

Dad looked thoughtfully at the road.

"Not yet. I figure the tourists don't know any more than I do, though. Why not just make stuff up?"

Dad was probably kidding, but it was hard to know for sure.

"Dad. You can't do that."

"Why not? Or, why not just tell all the passengers to figure out their own questions and then answer them? Why not tell them that their own natural curiosity is more important than me imposing my version of the truth on them?"

"Dad."

"In fact, why perpetuate the whole outdated, driver-run model of bus tours? Why not free ourselves of convention and let the passengers take the wheel if they want?"

I turned to look at Dad. "You don't want us to unschool, do you?"

"I didn't say that."

He had, though. That was how Dad said things.

Then he stopped the car in front of a long, gray building and we got out. Dad tried a couple of different keys and then opened up a door to the garage. I followed him inside, past rows of trucks, buses, and vans.

"Is that it?" I asked excitedly. I pointed to a bus that had a giant red lobster attached to the top, along with a sign that said MAINE ATTRACTIONS.

"No," said Dad. "That's someone else's tour bus. This one is ours."

He pointed to a smaller bus, painted red and white. It had a roof, but the windows had no glass. The open sides made me think of an old-fashioned trolley car, like from a movie I'd seen where a girl stood in one and sang about how her heart was zinging around.

Dad held an arm out like he was a lady presenting a prize on a TV game show we used to watch. That was years ago, before he and Mom had decided to get rid of the TV.

"There you have it. A genuine Portland, Maine, tour bus. Good for the transportation of large groups of wealthy, fact-hungry tourists."

I clapped my hands and jumped up and down, like I was a person who had just won the tour bus. That's what people on the show used to do, whenever they won something. It seemed they never already owned whatever it was they had just won.

"When can I start driving it around the city?" I asked in an excited prizewinner's voice.

"Not so fast, madam," Dad said, in a smooth game-show host voice. "First there is the small matter of cleaning it up."

He gestured for me to follow him back out to the car, where he popped open the trunk and took out a cardboard carton. It was full of rags and spray bottles.

"We have some work to do," Dad said in his normal voice.

"You didn't say anything about cleaning!" I pouted. I was just pretending to protest, though. I loved cleaning, and I couldn't

wait to brag to Zenith that I had been the one to get the bus all ready for business.

"But madam," Dad said in his host voice, "that's the most fantastic part of the prize! A trip for two to the fabulous interior of a dirty tour bus, complete with paper towels and cleaning fluid!"

"Yaaaay!" I yelled, jumping up and down again like I couldn't contain my delight.

We walked back into the garage and Dad set the box down in front of the bus. He rooted through his keys again and worked the bus door open. Then he held his arm out in a gallant, ladies-first gesture.

I climbed the steps and looked down the length of the aisle. I stopped short and felt my breath catch. I forgot all about joking around.

"Dad," I said. My voice shook. "You'd better come take a look at this."

Chapter 3

Unschool Colors

I heard Dad's steps as he climbed up behind me. I didn't turn around to face him. I couldn't take my eyes off of what I was seeing.

Someone had spray-painted angry words all across the side of the bus, just beneath the open space where the tourists would look out. GO HOME! LEAVE! STAY AWAY!, and some that were worse. For a second, I thought about the giant words hanging at Gabby's house. I shook my head to clear the confusion. These words didn't look anything like the ones Spirit had written. Spirit's words were encouraging. These were cruel.

Finally, I turned away. The red scrawl made my eyes hurt. I shut my lids and I saw cardboard boxes, piles of brown boxes filled with our stuff, waiting to move to a new town, a new business idea of Dad's, a new set of museums to visit, a new group of homeschool kids we would know for a while. I could see Mom's face, tense and resigned, and Zenith's, bitter and a little triumphant.

I opened my eyes and turned to Dad. He was shaking his head, his mouth drawn into line.

"Real nice welcome," he said. "Really, really nice."

"How did someone even get onto the bus?" I asked. "Aren't you the only one with a key?"

"As far as I know," Dad said. "But look at the open windows. Someone could have climbed up there, or been given a boost, and slipped in."

I walked toward the back of the bus, half worried that I would find something else. I wasn't sure what I was afraid of, exactly, but I did know that the sick feeling in my stomach would get even sicker until I knew for sure that the writing was the worst of it.

It was.

"Should we call the police?" I asked, walking back toward Dad. He stood with one hand on the driver's seat, surveying the damage.

Dad shook his head. "There's no point. This is a stupid prank someone pulled, probably some kids. The best thing for us to do is just clean it up."

He looked down at the box of paper towels and spray cleaner.

"This isn't going to do it," he admitted. "We're going to have to repaint."

"I don't mind painting," I said.

I told myself that I shouldn't feel so bad. Dad had said it was a stupid prank, and that was that. We would clean it up and Dad would start giving tours as planned.

But I couldn't shake the feeling that our time in Maine was ending rather than beginning—that the tour bus and unschooling were both about to join the list of experiments we'd tried, failed at, and left behind.

"What would you say to a trip to the paint store?" Dad asked.

I tried to summon the prizewinning lady of a few minutes ago.

"Yay!" I said, but Dad had forgotten that lady; he mistook me for a child still young enough to get excited about paint.

26

"That's the spirit," he said, and we spent the rest of the afternoon with brushes in hand, undoing the work of the vandals.

In the car on the way home, we were quiet. My back ached from the awkward angle I had held myself in, kneeling on a seat and reaching up with the brush. It felt like I'd spent half the time just moving tarps from seat to seat as I moved down my side of the bus. We didn't want to make matters worse by dripping paint on the seats.

"Do me a favor, Zale," Dad said, driving.

"Yeah?"

"Let me be the one to tell Mom and Zenith about the bus."

"Okay."

Once again I had been robbed of delivering a big scoop, but that didn't seem as important as it had the day before. I knew Dad wanted to say it in a way that sounded like it was no big deal. There were some lovely messages written in the bus, we could tell Mom, but we decided that it would be even more fun if we painted over them!

When we got home, Mom and Zenith were sitting at the dinner table. Dad shot me a look, like I was going to forget and blurt out the news. Both of us went to wash our hands, and then we sat down to eat.

"There you are!" said Mom. "How is the bus?"

Before Dad could say anything, Mom set a bowl of broccoli in front of me and said, "Well, I had something exciting happen today. I've been waiting until you got back to say anything."

Dad and I glanced at each other; should we wait?

Zenith hunched over her plate and ate steadily, as though none of us were there.

"What happened?" Dad asked.

"Well!" Mom said, leaning forward in her chair. Then she examined me more closely.

"Azalea, what happened to your shirt?"

I looked down. I hadn't realized that I was flecked with paint. We'd decided that it would be best to cover the scrawl in its own shade of red. I looked guiltily at Dad, and Mom followed my eyes.

"You, too!" she said. "Have you been painting? Or have you turned to a life of violent crime?"

"When we got to the bus," Dad said, "there was a little problem."

Mom's face set.

"I knew it. I knew that thing had to have problems. Why else did Jack sell it so cheap?"

Clearly this was not a new conversation for her and Dad. It was the wrong one for right now, though.

"That's not it," Dad told her. "Some kids got in with some spray paint, and we had to do some retouching."

Retouching? We'd spent the afternoon in there.

Mom wasn't fooled.

"What do you mean, some kids got in? How do you know it was kids?"

I didn't like where this was going. I preferred Dad's version of the story.

"Anyway, he didn't tell you what they spray-painted," I broke in. I told Mom and Zenith about the jeering messages, the angry red paint.

"That's awful," said Mom. She looked drawn and worried. "Why would someone do that?"

"It was just someone's idea of a joke," Dad said, spooning brown rice onto his plate. "It didn't mean anything."

"Wait a minute," I said, putting my fork down. "How did they know we were new in town?"

Somehow I imagined a "they," not just one person. Maybe they were a sneaky spray-painting gang who moved through the shadows of the city in cartoonish burglar masks, making trouble.

"Why did it say 'Go home' if it was just some random prank?"

Everyone, even Zenith, looked at Dad, waiting for an explanation.

"It didn't mean anything," he said unconvincingly through a mouthful of rice. He finished chewing and swallowed, then turned to Mom.

"Weren't you going to say something?" he asked. "Before we got on this topic?"

Mom studied Dad for a moment, as though she couldn't decide whether or not she was ready to move on from the subject of bus vandals. Then her face brightened a little.

"Yes," she said. "I have a piece of exciting news."

We all leaned forward to hear it.

"When I was in the supermarket today, I found a lady crying next to the sweet potatoes."

No one said anything. Sometimes with Mom, you just had to wait it out.

"She was having this sort of crisis, and no one else stopped to help her, but I did. I asked her if she needed to talk, and she did, and by the time we finished talking, she felt much better—like she could manage things again."

Mom beamed at us, and we glanced uneasily at one another.

Finally Dad prompted her. "And the exciting part is . . ."

"The exciting part is that I have decided to make use of the counseling degree I earned many eons ago, and start working with clients again," Mom said. "Now that the girls are unschooling, they don't need my time as much as they used to. I can see clients here in the house—just one or two at first, maybe, and then more. I'm going to be a life coach!"

Zenith dug a little hole in her rice with her fork, like a six-year-old.

"Don't you need to be a good swimmer for that?" she asked.

"Not a life*guard*," Mom told her, as though Zenith didn't already know. "A life coach. Someone who helps people strategize for their lives."

"This sweet potato lady," Dad said. "Is she going to be your first client?"

"Yes!" Mom told us excitedly.

I knew the rest of us were all thinking the same thing: Mom had a history of getting mixed up in people's lives and then regretting it. We all remembered Mrs. Briggs, who lived down the road from our orchard in Connecticut. Mom tried to reunite her with her long-lost brother, who turned out to be in prison for something too horrible to say.

"And how will you help this woman?" Dad asked.

"She's going to advise her to stay away from sweet potatoes," Zenith mumbled.

Dad laughed. I felt jealous that Zenith had gotten him to laugh, but I didn't think either of them was being very nice to Mom.

"Ha ha," Mom said, not smiling. "The great thing, of course, is that I will be working right here from home. Which means I need everybody to really pitch in to keep the house clean."

"How much are you going to charge your clients?" Dad asked. "Will they be paying you in root vegetables?"

Mom gave him a sharp look and stood up.

"Help me clear, girls," she said, and though we weren't quite finished eating, we did it.

Later that evening, Zenith and I lay on our beds, reading. Mom and Dad hadn't said too much after dinner was over, but they weren't yelling, either, so things probably weren't too bad.

I put my book aside so I could think about the tour bus.

"It was really scary," I told Zenith. I knew she would know what I was talking about.

"It was just paint," Zenith said, not taking her eyes from her book.

"You weren't there," I pointed out. "You don't know what it's like to get on a bus and see these giant letters, threatening you."

"They didn't threaten you, exactly," said Zenith. "They said to go away, but not that anything would happen if you didn't, right?"

I opened my mouth in a show of disbelief.

"Well, what do you *think* it meant?" I asked. "Go home now, or we'll throw you a nice party?"

Zenith pretended to read.

"Anyway," I told her, "I've been thinking about it. I don't believe this was just some random prank, like Dad says."

I paused, so that Zenith would get the full effect of what was coming next.

"I think I know who did it."

Now I had her attention.

"Remember what Mom said about Dad's friend who sold him the bus? How she found out about the unschooling meeting through him, because his niece is an unschooler?"

"Yeah?" Zenith had a look on her face like I was crazy. Like I was the kind of person you would find weeping in the produce department.

"I met his niece at the party. Nola? She was that girl dressed completely in pink?"

"So?"

"So, she hated me. She's good friends with that girl, Gabby, and she saw that Gabby and I became friends right away, and she hates me for it. She wouldn't let me dance with them."

Now that I'd said it aloud, it sounded sort of stupid. I was glad I'd left out the part about the Secret Squid Sisters.

Zenith folded her pillow in half and stuck it behind her head to prop herself up higher.

"So you think this Nola zipped home from the party, bought some red spray paint—probably because the store was out of pink—asked her mom for a ride to the garage, climbed onto our bus, spray-painted it, and then told her mom she was ready to go home?"

"Yes," I said firmly. "That's what I think. More or less. Unless you have a better theory."

"Not a one," said Zenith, lifting her book in front of her face to signal that the conversation was over.

But I wasn't giving up that easily. I wanted this tour bus business of ours to work. I wanted us to finally, finally stay in one place. And if I was unschooling now, that meant I was in charge of what I learned.

And I planned to learn who vandalized our bus.

Chapter 4

Unschool Playground

A few mornings later, Dad made his famous whole-grain pancakes. I ate many of them, and quickly.

Gabby and her mother were coming over, and they were going to take me to the park and then back to Gabby's house. It was my first time getting together with Gabby since we had met at the unschool meeting, and I was sure we were going to be good friends.

"So, today," I asked Mom, cramming in a bite of pancake, "are Gabby and I supposed to be playing, or, you know, unschooling?"

"That's just it!" Mom said. "There's no distinction. Or there shouldn't be. Children learn in all sorts of ways. Playing can be learning, and learning can be playing."

"Oh," I said, pretending that this cleared things right up.

It didn't much matter, anyway. Mostly, I just wanted to tell Gabby about the tour bus. I wasn't sure if I should tell her that I suspected Nola. They *were* friends, after all, as hard as it was for me to believe. Still, Nola was my number-one suspect, and if she was the guilty party, Gabby would find out eventually. It might even be an act of kindness to tell her now, rather than later.

Dad took a final swallow of coffee and pushed his chair back from the table.

"I'm off," he said. "I'm doing the first practice run today."
He held up his map of the city.

A week ago I would have been disappointed that I couldn't go
along, but I was so happy about seeing Gabby that I didn't care
very much.

"Good luck," I said. "Don't get lost!"

Zenith hit me with one of her famous eye rolls—it was surprising how much contempt she could pack into one—and turned
to Mom.

"Can I ask you something?"

"Of course," Mom said. She set down her coffee mug and
waited.

"You know how I like math?" Zenith asked.

"Yes?"

"I want to go to school to learn it better."

Mom sat up straight.

"I don't understand. Why would you want to do that?"

Zenith waved her hands, explaining. "I'm using these books
you got me, and they're not that great. I mean, they're okay,
but I need a person who can explain it to me. Better than you
and Dad, I mean," she added uncharitably. Zenith had long ago
surpassed their comfort level with math.

"I saw online that the high school has summer classes, and I
want to take one."

Mom put her hands on the table and tried to look reasonable.
I knew she didn't feel that way. Neither Zenith nor I had ever
been to school, and Mom thought that was for the best. She had
hated school as a kid. She thought the whole idea of it—a bunch
of kids being led by a teacher, told what to learn and how to
learn it—was all wrong.

"It would just be one class," Zenith explained. "I wouldn't really be in school. I would still be homeschooling. Unschooling."

As Mom worked on a response, the doorbell rang. I hopped up and ran to answer the door.

It was Gabby and Spirit.

"Come on in!" I yelled, opening the door wide. Gabby rushed in and threw her arms around me.

"Hey, Squid Sister!" she said. She stepped back, and I said hi to Spirit.

"Hello, hello!" Spirit said, spreading her arms to include everyone in the room.

There was something funny about the way she and Gabby looked, but I couldn't quite put my finger on it. Then I realized: they were wearing matching scarves, large hairy ones swirling with rich shades of blue and purple. It was a bit late in the season for scarves, I thought. Maybe these were more for decoration than bad weather.

"What beautiful scarves!" Mom said, a step ahead of me.

"Thank you," Spirit replied. "We made them ourselves last year."

"We had a textile phase," added Gabby.

"It's such a fascinating journey," murmured Spirit.

Mom nodded as though she agreed.

"My journey is going to include a math class at the high school," Zenith announced. She looked Spirit in the eye and smiled, waiting to see her reaction.

"My!" Spirit told her. "What an interesting choice. I'm sure it will be eye-opening."

She tucked one end of her scarf behind her shoulder.

"Well, we haven't quite finished discussing that," Mom said. "Anyway," she continued in a loud, bright voice, "it's wonderful to see you. Would you like to sit down and have some tea before you head out? Coffee?"

"I wonder what the teacher will be like," Zenith continued.

"The coffee is all ready, but I can make some tea in about three seconds."

"And the other students," Zenith said. "I wonder if it will be helpful to have a large group learning at the same time as me."

"Or maybe something cold?" Mom went on. "Some iced tea?"

"You can't ignore this," Zenith told her.

Spirit glided over to Mom and gave her a small, one-armed hug.

"I'll have to take a pass on that lovely offer of tea. We have too much learning to do! We'll just take Azalea and be on our merry way."

She headed to the door and Gabby and I, relieved, followed her out into the fresh morning air.

We slid into the backseat of Spirit's car and pulled on our seat belts. The car was different from ours. It was very, very clean on the inside. And riding in it felt very smooth and quiet. I wanted to think this over, but Gabby spoke.

"You know, there are all kinds of ways to unschool. You can tell your mom. It's not like there's a rule that Zenith can't take a class if she wants."

"I'll tell her," I said. "We're totally new at this. I think she's afraid we're already doing it wrong."

"There's no wrong way, Azalea," Spirit called from the front seat.

I tried to think of something to say for an answer, but we'd arrived at the park.

Spirit pulled the car over in front of the playground and we climbed out.

"Come on," Gabby said, and led me down a small hill to the play area. There were no other kids there. Spirit settled herself with a book at a picnic table.

"Let's go on this thing." Gabby climbed up a small staircase. It was on the little structure meant for young children.

"I think we might be too old for this one," I said.

"Only if you accept society's strict and arbitrary designations for how people of different ages should behave. Explore the world however you see fit, Azalea!"

She tucked her scarf behind one shoulder, and I realized she was deliberately, accurately imitating Spirit. I laughed, and so did Gabby.

"She's right, though," Gabby continued, her face turning more serious. "I mean, who says eleven-year-olds can't play on a small slide? Or, for that matter, play in sandboxes, or learn Latin, or design bridges?"

I lifted my foot to the top of a tiny slide. I felt like a giant. I pulled the other foot up, and stood tall.

"I don't think I'd want to cross any bridge designed by me," I said. "I think I'd rather cross a Zenith bridge."

"Come this way!" Gabby said, racing across to another part of the playground and leaping up to grab a horizontal bar. She hung suspended for a minute, and then dropped down.

I could see she was a little awkward on the bar. I didn't want to show off, but I couldn't help myself. I grabbed hold and swung my feet up, then let them drop behind my head. Maybe Gabby knew all about unschooling, and lived in a big house with a yard and had a quiet car, but I was good at gymnastics.

"Skin the cat," I explained to Gabby, as the blood rushed to my head. That was the name of the move I was doing. I didn't know why a perfectly good move had such a disgusting name.

"Wow," she said. "I totally cannot do stuff like that."

"Sure you can," I told her. "I'll show you."

Gabby was right, though. She really couldn't do stuff like that. She struggled for a while, trying to kick her legs backward, until finally she rested, dangling from the bar. I dangled beside her.

"Don't worry about it," I said. "I bet you'll get better with practice."

"That's what I told myself about modern dance," Gabby said. "I've been doing it for two years and I'm still the worst one in the group!"

"So why do you do it?"

"Because I love it!" Gabby said happily. Sunlight streamed down around us, and I decided that if this was unschooling, I liked it.

Then I remembered about the bus. Here I was, acting like unschooling was one big day at the park, when I was supposed to be solving a mystery. I needed to tell Gabby about the tour bus, and maybe my idea about Nola.

It was a risk, though, the part about Nola. I didn't want Gabby to get angry with me. But I also didn't want Nola ruining our tour bus business so that we had to move away. Maybe Gabby would remember some little thing Nola had said about the bus, some clue that might point to her as the culprit.

Before I could say anything, though, Gabby dropped down off the bar.

Spirit got up from her bench and walked over to us.

"Lovely!" she called. "Gabby, this reminds me of how you first learned about gravity!"

I dropped to the ground and looked at Gabby.

She shook her head. "Bicycle. Crutches. Don't ask."

A preschooler shot in front of us, the first kid we'd seen at the playground, besides us.

His mother followed close behind. She looked at us and sized up the situation: two big girls at the playground in the middle of the day.

"No school today?" the mother asked.

"We don't go to school," Gabby said.

I glanced at Spirit, who smiled broadly but said nothing.

"You must be homeschooled," the mother suggested.

Her son slid down the tiny slide and threw his arms up in triumph.

"No," I told her. "We unschool."

I glanced at Spirit, who was still watching us, beaming. She caught my eye and her smile widened. The little boy gave up on the slide and edged over to our bar, stretching his hands toward it.

The mother still wanted to get to the bottom of this.

"What does it mean to unschool?" she asked.

Spirit trilled her fingers at the preschooler, who was looking at her scarf.

"It means we learn on our own, not in school," Gabby offered.

"Oh," the mother said. "So, homeschooled."

She glanced at her son, who had turned to stare at Gabby's scarf. Gabby held out the end of it for the child to touch.

"No. Homeschool is a type of school," I explained to the mother. "Your mom or dad is the teacher, and you do lessons and stuff. Unschool is different."

I felt like there was more that I was supposed to say. I pretended I was Gabby, imitating Spirit.

"It's a natural, child-driven exploration of the world," I finished.

Spirit, watching, gave a tiny nod, and I felt pleased.

"I see," said the mother. The little boy took off across the playground, and the mother scooted after him.

"Bye, girls," she called. We waved.

"That was weird," I said.

"Get used to it," Gabby replied.

She climbed a small staircase and stepped onto a rope bridge.

"You're going to have that conversation about a million more times."

I climbed up after her. I was glad I was at the playground with Gabby and not Zenith. Zenith would have parked herself on a bench, folding her arms around herself, too old to have any fun. If she owned a phone, she would be one of those girls jabbing at it like she had some secret important life elsewhere, but my parents wouldn't get her one—a big sore spot with her. I didn't know who she thought she would be keeping in touch with, anyway. Neither of us had made any close friends in Connecticut, and North Carolina felt like forever ago.

Gabby and I danced on the rope bridge, making it swing wildly.

"I don't get why people have so much trouble with the difference between homeschool and unschool," I complained, as though I hadn't just been one of those people. "*Home. Un.* It's two different things."

Gabby nodded her agreement. "It's true. I mean, you wouldn't call, like, being homesick being *un*sick. You wouldn't call someone *home*happy instead of unhappy. It's two totally different things."

"You wouldn't call underwear *home*derwear," I said, and we laughed until we had to lie down on the bridge. Then we fell out the sides, so we knew that the laws of gravity were still in working order.

"Come check this out!" Gabby pointed toward a large metal drum.

We picked ourselves up from the ground and ran over to it. Gabby selected two big sticks from the grass and handed one to me.

"Listen!" She banged the drum with her stick, a deep, hollow sound. "Now you!"

I pounded away on the drum for a while before I remembered about Nola and the bus.

This was something I had begun to notice about unschooling. With so many choices, it was easy to forget to finish what you started.

I decided to pretend that I was still homeschooling, and that Mom had assigned me the task of finding out who had vandalized the bus: "Here's an idea to explore, Azalea," she would say. "Let me know what you come up with."

I dropped my stick. Spirit had returned to her picnic bench, too far away to hear.

"I have something to tell you," I said.

Gabby continued drumming. She couldn't hear me over the racket. This was not a good start.

"Gabby!" I shouted.

Finally she looked at me and noticed that I wasn't drumming. She dropped her stick.

I began again. "I want to tell you about something. Yesterday this crazy thing happened. My dad bought this tour bus—"

"From Nola's uncle," Gabby broke in. "I know. She told me all about it."

Aha!

"So we went out to see it, my dad and me," I continued. "And we got on and there were all these words painted on it!"

Gabby's mouth dropped open a little. "What kinds of words?"

"Stuff like 'Go away. Go home.' "

"Oh." Gabby looked a little disappointed.

"It was really scary," I explained. "The words were red and very big." I paused. "Menacing."

Now Gabby's face looked properly horrified. "What did you do?"

"What *could* we do? We got some paint and covered them up. My dad is going out today to do his first test run of his tour route."

"You didn't call the police?"

"My dad said it was just some kids." I paused. "You don't think . . ."

Gabby waited, not helping me out.

"I mean, it's kind of weird that it said "Go home,' like it was someone who knows we just moved here. Someone who doesn't like us. Or me."

Gabby either pretended not to understand me, or she really didn't.

"I mean, I'm just wondering who would . . ."

And then the conversation was over, because who should come barreling onto the playground but Nola herself, resplendent in a pink ski jacket and pink leggings.

"Gabbers!" Nola bellowed, speeding toward us.

I saw a woman sitting with Spirit at the picnic bench—Nola's mother, probably. She was dressed all in white. I wondered if each person in that family had a signature color, or what.

"Hey, Nole," said Gabby.

When Nola reached us, they hugged.

"Spirit said you might come," said Gabby.

This was the first I'd heard of it. I wondered why Gabby hadn't mentioned anything to me. I told myself I wouldn't have come if I'd known that Nola would be there.

"And here I am!" cried Nola, spreading her pink arms.

"You remember my friend Azalea," Gabby said.

It was another one of those times where she sounded more like an adult than a child. I didn't mind it, though. It seemed normal for her.

"Yes, I do," said Nola, not looking at me. "Let's go on the seesaw!"

The seesaw sat two on each side. The little boy and his mother were taking up one seat on each side, but when they saw Nola flying toward them, they got up and left. Nola plopped herself on one of the seats and pointed across the way for Gabby.

"Sit," she commanded.

Gabby sat in the back-most seat, sending Nola upward.

"You sit, too," Gabby told me. "There's plenty of room."

"No, thanks," I said, and started to walk back toward the drum.

"I don't really feel like doing this, either," Gabby said. "I'm getting hungry. Aren't we all going back to my house for lunch?"

So it wasn't enough that my secret return to homeschooling hadn't worked out. Now the rest of the afternoon was ruined, too. I wondered if I should say I felt sick, and ask Spirit to take me home. If I did, though, Mom would be full of questions, and Zenith would laugh at me.

Besides, this was the perfect chance to make the transition for real to unschooling. No assignments from Mom, no reports to give. Just me and my natural, child-driven exploration of the world.

First challenge: explore how to get along with my least favorite person, Nola the Pink.

Chapter 5

Unschool Lunch

At Gabby's house, things just got worse.

Spirit collected some papers from the kitchen counter and announced that she and Nola's mother had to go into her office and make a chart about water pollutants. So it would be just Gabby, Nola, and me, best buddies, for the entire afternoon.

"I thought you were making us pizza," Gabby complained as Spirit swept past her.

"I was going to," Spirit said, "but I forgot to do the dough, and then I remembered about this. You can make lunch for yourself and the other girls, Gabby. It'll be fun!"

No, it wouldn't. Except . . . maybe this wasn't such a bad thing. Maybe this was my chance to find out more about Nola, to see if she let anything slip about the bus.

"It's the old bait and switch!" Gabby said. "No fair."

"The old what?" I asked.

"Bait and switch. Like when you're lured in by the promise of one thing, but then it gets switched around on you. Like you think you're going to get pizza, and you end up having to make yourself a peanut butter sandwich. It's the oldest trick in the book."

Nola danced around the kitchen like she owned it, singing a high-pitched song and swinging Gabby around square-dance style. My afternoon with Gabby: my life's most recent bait and switch.

Gabby fixed the sandwiches while Nola squawked and jabbered about a movie she planned to see, not pausing for breath and not acknowledging my presence.

I tried to use the time to plot out how I would uncover her secret, but I couldn't think of anything. Maybe if she would just stop talking for half a second, I could think better. I almost wished Zenith were there. She was good at problem solving. Except, of course, that she had been no help whatsoever on the subject of the bus.

Gabby plopped a plate with a sandwich in front of each of us, and there was a welcome silence while everyone ate. When we finished, Gabby asked us what we wanted to do. Nola was still chewing, so I had a chance to say something.

"Maybe play in the yard?" I suggested. I remembered it from when we had come to the meeting, and I wanted to get a better look. I thought maybe I had seen a tire swing.

"I thought we could do one of our projects," Nola told Gabby, her mouth still a little full, as though I had said nothing. She swallowed the rest of her sandwich. "Maybe work on the undersea exploration."

Gabby explained it to me. "I've been really interested in mollusks, and Nola has been studying the effects of water pollution on sea life. Our mothers are part of a group that monitors pollution in the ocean, and we got interested in it, too. So we've been sort of putting together what we learn into a big model."

"It's not just a model," corrected Nola. This was the closest she'd come yet to actually talking to me. "It's a multidimensional exploration. There's sounds and images and textures."

"I did something like that once when I was homeschooling," I said. "It was about outer space. I made this big model."

Nola giggled. "Like, with foam balls?"

My face burned. What was wrong with foam balls? Besides, I'd also used an inflated balloon for the sun, and lentils for the planets' moons.

"Very *school*," Nola told Gabby, who looked down at the floor.

Then Gabby said, "I don't feel like working on the exploration right now. I feel like playing on the tire swing."

I smiled at Gabby as she led the way to the backyard, grateful that she'd read my mind.

Nola followed, her hands on her hips. She stood like that while Gabby told me to climb onto the swing and gave me a push. Gabby and I took turns swinging for a while, and then the back door opened and two boys came into the yard. One of them was Gibran, Gabby's brother. The other boy looked the same age as Gibran, but skinnier, with darker hair.

"Azalea, you met my brother, Gibran. And that's Nola's brother, Charlie."

I gave a shy wave, and the boys nodded and grunted as they walked over to a tarp in front of a large shed in the corner of the yard. I noticed that Nola's brother wore blue jeans and a green shirt, so maybe the one-color thing was just for the women in the family.

"Oh, God, not the boat," said Nola. She did me a great favor by addressing me. "They've been working on that boat for, like, ever."

"I know," I said coolly, so she wouldn't think I cared that she was talking to me. I remembered Gabby telling me that her brother was building a boat.

"It's never going to float," complained Nola. "And besides, they won't let us help."

"Which is too bad," Gabby said loudly, so the boys could hear. "Because we would make excellent helpers."

"And if *we* were making a boat," Nola added, even louder, "*we* would let *them* help."

The boys ignored them.

Nola's brother yanked the tarp off. Several long wooden planks lay on another tarp beneath. I tried to imagine what they would look like as a boat. All I could see was separate pieces. I couldn't imagine how they would fit together to make something whole and solid.

My life felt like that, sometimes.

I thought about how it would be to move yet again. We would pack up everything we owned, I would take a last look at our apartment, and a neighbor would hand us a cake or a houseplant as a going-away gift. This time, though, it wouldn't just be a neighbor I had to leave behind. It would be Gabby, my friend.

Then we would start over. There would be a new town, a new apartment. Dad would start out with high hopes for his latest idea. Then, the early optimism would give way. There would be some problem that could not have been foreseen: a bad economy; an ill-timed frost; a city that refused to accessorize its gerbils.

No. I wasn't leaving this time. I had a friend here—I was happy. I was not moving again.

A thought struck me: what if I could get Nola to like me?

Suppose I couldn't prove that she was the bus vandal. Suppose she was too sneaky for that. What if I took away her motive to drive my family out of town? Would she—assuming she was the culprit—keep harming the bus if she *liked* me?

There was no way I was backing off my friendship with Gabby. That was for sure. If she was jealous of Gabby's and my friendship, well, I couldn't help that. And the truth was, I would probably never like Nola all that much.

I didn't have to, though. I just had to get *her* to like *me*. Enough, at least, so she wouldn't want to expel me from the state.

I could do this.

"I have an idea," I told Gabby and Nola. My mind raced. I glanced toward the boys and then back at Nola and Gabby. "Let's make them something to drink."

Gabby looked surprised. "Like lemonade?"

"Kind of like lemonade," I said. "But not."

Nola looked at me with a flicker of interest. "What did you have in mind?"

"Switchel," I announced. "It's a beverage that field hands in New England drank in the olden days. Because they thought drinking plain cold water was harmful, they made a drink called switchel. The lady of the house would bring big jugs of it out to the fields and the workers would drink it."

"You like history!" Gabby cried. "Me, too!"

"We homeschoolers—former homeschoolers—have been known to read a book or two," I replied. "Not to mention the ten million museums, historic houses, and old-time reenactment villages I've been to."

"So, just what's in this switchel?" asked Nola.

I could tell she was sizing me up, trying to figure out my angle. Was I hatching a scheme to get back at the boys, or was I just suggesting we make old-timey refreshments?

I raised my eyebrows slyly.

"Oh, water, vinegar, hot ginger powder, some other delicious stuff."

Nola smiled. "Perfect."

"Then we're agreed," I said. "Switchel for the boys it is."

We trooped back into the kitchen and Gabby peered into a cabinet.

"Tell me again what we need?"

I couldn't tell if Gabby cared about seeking revenge against the boys, or if she was just going along with Nola and me. From what I had seen of Gabby's kindheartedness, she might not even understand that switchel *was* a revenge plan. She might think it was just a nice treat for them.

Spirit swirled into the kitchen and reached past Gabby to find a box of crackers.

"What are you girls up to?" she asked.

"Oh, we're doing a sort of history project," Nola told her.

Spirit nodded and left with her crackers.

"First, we'll need a jug," Nola announced.

Gabby shut the cabinet and checked around the kitchen, finally pulling an empty plastic milk jug from the recycling bin.

"Now fill it partway with water," Nola dictated.

She seemed to have taken command of the project. I didn't care, even though it was all my idea. The important thing was that she was enjoying herself. If she was going to be that easy to figure out, she and I could get along just fine. In fact, maybe I could do more than just get along with her. Maybe I could get her to say something about the bus.

Gabby turned the cold-water tap on, rinsed the jug, and then filled it three-quarters of the way.

"Now the ingredients," Nola said, turning to me. "What goes in first?"

"Molasses," I said with authority.

Gabby pulled a chair over to a cabinet and climbed up.

"I think there's some sugar and stuff way back here. Spirit likes to use sweeteners sparingly." She started rummaging. "Aha! I found the sugar. I knew that was in there somewhere. Will that work?"

"Keep looking," Nola said. "We need molasses for this recipe."

She turned to me with a wicked smile. I gave her one back.

"Are you sure?" Gabby asked. "Have you ever had molasses?"

I could tell by her voice that she had, and she didn't like it. She seemed to have momentarily forgotten—if she'd ever understood—the point of the plan.

Nola smiled knowingly. "Yes. And yes."

If I was going to say something about the bus, I had to just do it. I couldn't wait around for the conversation to shift spontaneously to the subject of tourist attractions.

"So, Nola," I said, while Gabby looked through the cabinet, "your uncle used to give bus tours?"

My voice sounded too loud. Nola's lids lowered slightly, signaling her lack of interest in the topic.

"That's right," she said.

"Got it!" Gabby said, handing down a small bottle filled with dark brown syrup, and then climbing off the chair.

"Let me see it," I said, taking the bottle. I twisted the top off and sniffed. It was sweet and bitter at the same time, like a medicine that's supposed to taste good to kids, but doesn't.

"Ick," I said, and handed it back to Nola.

She dipped a finger into the bottle and tasted it. She grimaced. "Perfect. The boys will love it."

"About a quarter cup," I announced, like I made switchel every day.

Gabby measured the molasses into a metal cup. I watched the thick syrup fold on itself in layers as it poured.

"Do you have a funnel?" Nola asked Gabby.

Gabby pointed to a drawer near me. I opened it, found a funnel, and handed it to Nola. I tried to think of something else to say about the bus, something incredibly clever that would trap her into a confession.

"So, tours, huh?"

Nola held the funnel to the top of the jug and tipped the molasses in.

"This could take a while," she said. "Meantime, Gabby, find the vinegar."

"Are you sure about that?" Gabby asked, wincing a little. "It doesn't have to be completely authentic, you know."

"Oh, yes it does!" Nola assured her. "Besides, the boys deserve something special, and what could be more delicious and refreshing than vinegar?"

"Vinegar it is!" said Gabby.

The vinegar was on a lower shelf than the molasses, so she didn't need a chair to get it out. She set it on the counter and unscrewed the cap. I got a whiff of it without trying. It was a sour, awful smell.

"In it goes!" sang Nola, and, removing the molasses funnel, she poured great glugs of it into the switchel jug.

"I feel sorry for those field hands," I said. "All those hours working in the hot sun, and this is their reward."

I hated to admit it, but I was starting to enjoy myself a little, too. I didn't even mind much that my investigation was going nowhere.

"Nonsense," said Nola. "It's delightful."

She added an extra shot of vinegar to the mixture. "They'll love it."

"And finally, the ginger," Gabby said. "I remember reading about this. People used to think it was good for the workers' stomachs."

She opened a different cabinet and examined a spice rack. Each little compartment had a different type of spice in a glass container.

"I keep telling Spirit to alphabetize these, but she says she has a system. Here! Ginger."

She pulled out a little round jar and tossed it to Nola, who caught it.

"Maybe a teaspoon," Gabby told Nola.

"Or maybe a little more," I said.

"Coming up."

Nola opened the container and looked at the yellow powder inside. She wet a finger with her tongue and stuck it in, then tasted the powder.

"Weird," she said. "Hot." She opened the lid and poured a lot into the jug.

"That's way more than a teaspoon!" Gabby cried.

"Is it?" asked Nola innocently. "Well, it will be that much better for their stomachs."

I opened a couple of drawers until I found a long wooden spoon.

"Mixing time!" I said. The top of the jug was too narrow for the spoon, so I stuck the handle in and stirred.

Gabby got out three small glasses.

"Wait—let's add just a dash more ginger," said Nola. She shook the container over the jug.

"That's enough!" said Gabby. "It'll be way too hot."

"That would be such a shame," said Nola.

She managed one more shake before Gabby yanked the container away. Then Gabby poured a tiny bit of the liquid into each glass.

"Ladies," Gabby said, "a toast! To the beverages of other centuries!"

I picked up my glass and clinked it against Gabby's. "To switchel!"

Nola clinked both our glasses. "To giving hardworking people exactly what they deserve."

I laughed.

We all took a sip. I sputtered and spat mine back out.

"Nola, you put way too much ginger in this," I said. My eyes were tearing. "This is extra terrible."

Nola savored hers thoughtfully.

"I disagree," she said. "It has a nice kick."

But I could see that her eyes were watering, too.

Gabby took a second sip of hers. She didn't flinch.

"This is either incredibly great or completely awful. I haven't decided yet."

"I'm going with awful," I said.

"Get a couple of clean glasses," Nola ordered Gabby. "I'll carry the jug."

We went outside and walked over to the shed where the boys were standing with their backs to us, looking at their pile of boards and a large blueprint that lay next to it. They seemed to be trying to figure something out. The air was cool and damp, and they didn't exactly look like field hands dying for a drink. Still, Nola called out to them.

"Hey, guys," she said. "You look like you could use a little refreshment. We made some lemonade."

"It's actually switch—" Gabby started to say, but Nola turned around and shushed her.

"It's basically lemonade," Nola said. She took one of the glasses from Gabby and poured some. "Gibran? Want some?"

"Maybe later," he said, his back still turned. He knelt down and fiddled with the boards. "This one needs to be, like, up against here," he said to Charlie.

Nola didn't give up.

"Charlie, you must be thirsty. How about it?"

She held out the glass to her brother. He took a sip, grimaced, and handed the glass back to Nola.

"What is this stuff?" he asked.

"It's just a delicious old recipe we know about," Gabby told him, and the three of us looked at each other. I saw that Gabby had understood the plan all along. A laugh bubbled up in me; I couldn't help it. I gave a sort of snort. That made Nola snort, too. Maybe it wasn't so crazy to think that she and I could be friends.

"I don't think the sides are going to line up with the transom," Gibran said to Charlie, like we weren't even there.

"I know," Charlie agreed. "Something looks wrong."

"Delicious beverage, anyone?" Nola asked. "Gibran?"

She rocked Charlie's drinking glass so the switchel swirled around in it. It looked pretty good, if you didn't know what it tasted like.

"Nola," Charlie said, "hold the transom up for us."

Nola didn't think twice before going over to the enemy. She set down the glass and the jug and grabbed the board he was pointing at.

"Here?"

"Yeah. Just keep that steady so we can see how the sides fit next to it."

"Got it," she said, crouching down and gripping the board—and just like that, she was one of the field hands.

Gabby and I, fine ladies still, stood watching while Charlie and Gibran wrestled with the sides of the boat.

This wasn't going the way I wanted. I needed it to be the way it had started out: the girls united on one side, the boys on the other. The whole point of this was for Nola and me to be on the same side.

"If they don't want our switchel," I said loudly, "we can just take it back inside. Right, girls?"

Nola continued holding the board. I had ceased, once again, to exist.

I bent to pick up the jug that Nola had set down.

"Last chance!" I sang, swirling the liquid around like Nola had. "Doesn't it look tempting?" I gave the jug an extra, emphatic jerk, and some of the switchel sloshed down the side. A large drop of it landed on the blueprint.

"I'm sorry!" I said. As I quickly stepped away from the paper, I kicked over the glass Nola had put on the ground. A dark stain spread across the boat plans.

"Oh, nice work," said Gibran, dragging the blueprint across the grass, away from me. "It's all wet now. Gabby, would you get your friends away from here?"

"Yeah, nice going, Azalea," Nola said, one hand on her hip. "Way to be helpful."

She didn't move when Gabby and I turned to go back to the house.

"So much for the revenge plan," I said, setting the jug on the kitchen counter. "It didn't work at all."

Nothing had worked. Not my attempt to find out what Nola knew about the bus, and certainly not my stupid idea about getting her to like me so that she'd stop trying to make my family leave. Now she hated me more than ever. I wasn't any too fond of her, myself.

"I know!" agreed Gabby. "Nola totally changed sides!"

She put the glasses next to the jug on the counter.

"The old bait and switchel," I said. "It's the oldest trick in the book."

We shook our heads solemnly. Then I raised the jug to salute her and she raised one of the glasses back. We tipped the liquid ceremoniously into the sink and watched it swirl down the drain.

Chapter 6
Unschool Library

It was time to step up the sleuth work.

Someone out there had vandalized our bus, and whether or not it was Nola, I was going to find out who had done it. Anyway, that was what the feisty kids in novels always resolved to do, and it seemed to work out for them. So when Gabby and I arranged to meet downtown at the library a week later, I had a plan.

Mom dropped me off in front of the library's sliding doors and I ran inside. The public library was always one of our first stops in a new town, so I was already familiar with this one.

I found Gabby easily. She was sitting at a table, looking at a book about the history of modern dance. The book was open to a page with a photo of a dancer making herself into the shape of a chair. I wondered if Gabby did this with her dance group.

"Guess what?" I said, careful to keep my voice at a library-appropriate level.

Gabby looked up from her book. "What?"

"We have a mystery to solve!"

Gabby slammed the book shut. "Where do we start?"

This seemed a little abrupt. "Don't you want to know the mystery?"

"I figured it was the bus. Don't we want to know who wrote that stuff in the bus?"

"Yeah," I said.

I tried to think of something more dramatic to add, but I couldn't.

"That's it. And I have a plan." I waved my arm at the books all around us. "We're going to do some research."

"What?"

"Research. We're going to read everything we can about tour buses. The history of tour buses in Portland. People who have operated tour buses here. Whatever's going on here, we're going to get to the bottom of it."

I wondered if I should mention Nola. I wasn't as sure about her as I'd been before, but I still had my suspicions. Maybe it would be better if I didn't say anything outright to Gabby—at least, not until I felt more sure. In any case, it was time to broaden the search.

"Where is all this information going to be?" Gabby asked, looking around. "In the tour bus section of the library?"

"Very funny."

Gabby stood up and pulled her empty canvas library bag over her shoulder.

"Listen, Azalea: you're right about needing to do research about tour buses—but not here. Come with me."

"What?"

"We've got to figure out who would want to force you out of here."

She was already halfway between our table and the library entrance.

I followed her across the lobby. "Where are we going?" I asked.

The glass doors of the building slid open and we stepped out into the humid summer air. A few teenagers lounged sullenly on the grass beneath a statue across the street, and I wondered if Zenith, caught up in her new school life, her new teenaged self, would join them one day soon.

"We're going," Gabby announced, "on a spying mission."

Did she suspect Nola, too?

"Who exactly are we spying on?"

"The competition," Gabby pronounced darkly.

I trailed her across the street, and we worked our way down the brick sidewalks, through the part of the city called the Old Port, where there were lots of shops and shoppers.

We headed toward the harbor, where boats carried fisher-men, tourists, and passengers to the islands in Casco Bay. Dad's pickup and drop-off spot, which came with the bus, was right in the busiest part, in front of the sidewalk by the ferry terminal. A nearby walkway led to a pier stretching into the water. Just behind the shops and restaurants, boats bobbed in the harbor. Seagulls strutted around, wrestling with bits of food and trash on the sidewalk.

"The thing is," Gabby explained as we walked, dodging par-ents pushing strollers and young couples holding ice-cream cones, "there's only one theory that really makes sense. And that's that someone else who runs tours is scared of the compe-tition."

She looked over at me in triumph while I thought this over.

"You might be right," I said slowly.

It did make sense that someone currently running tours would want us to leave. Maybe it made a lot more sense than my theory about Nola. But I had a feeling, still, and I wasn't ready to let it go.

We stopped to listen to a street musician playing a fiddle.

"I wish I could do that!" said Gabby. "I need to learn how to play an instrument."

She dug through her pockets and pulled out a dollar bill, which she laid carefully in the fiddle case among a scattering of coins.

We continued walking.

Why not say something about Nola, I thought. *Nothing outright. Just a tiny hint to steer Gabby in the right direction.*

I gathered up my resolve.

"I wonder if there could be another possibility, besides a competing tour company."

"What?" Gabby hummed a version of the fiddle tune to herself.

"Well, what if someone here just doesn't like us? Someone who wants us to leave town?"

Gabby stopped her humming and laughed.

"That's silly. No one would just want you to go away, unless they feared for their business. That's why we're going to start checking out the other tour buses. See if we can figure anything out."

At least now I knew that her theory had nothing to do with Nola. I decided to keep quiet about that for a while. Maybe Gabby was on to something with this competition business. It was worth looking into.

I pointed to a sign with a picture of a tour bus on it.

"This is Dad's pickup spot!" I told Gabby. "This is his sign!"

Dad had given his very first tour just the day before. I had begged him to let Gabby, Zenith, and me come along, but he wanted us to wait until everything was running smoothly. The first day had been, in his words, not a total disaster. I hoped today would be even better for him.

"Okay, so isn't there another tour company that picks up somewhere right near here?" asked Gabby. "The one with the huge lobster statue on top of the bus?"

"Yeah. It picks up on a side street." I pointed. "All the way down there."

"Let's go," said Gabby.

I felt a little sad as we left Dad's spot. People were just walking by, like it was any old place on the sidewalk. Worse, they were probably heading for the lobster bus. They probably thought that a tour bus with a statue of an enormous, grinning sea creature on top gave better tours than one that didn't. Maybe they were right.

"Okay," Gabby said as we approached.

The bus was pulled up to the curb, the door shut, the driver waiting inside. The giant lobster clung to the roof like it intended to eat the bus.

"Just act natural—like we're thinking about taking the tour."

I tried to think what a person who wanted to take a tour felt like. Curious? Lost? I looked around, wide-eyed, like I had just arrived from someplace entirely different, a thousand miles from an ocean. I smelled the sea in the air. I was glad I lived in Portland.

Gabby found the ticket seller, a lady sitting on a stool outside the bus. A sign next to her said MAINE ATTRACTIONS. The lady made change for a small herd of tourists and handed them each a ticket from an envelope.

"Boarding in three minutes," she told them.

"How much for tickets?" Gabby asked.

The lady gazed past her. "Ten each."

Gabby and I did not have twenty dollars. I signaled Gabby by lifting my eyebrows: *now what?* But Gabby was unfazed.

"So what would you say makes this tour special?" Gabby asked the woman.

I remembered how she'd shaken my hand the first time I met her, the way she had of seeming very grown-up sometimes.

"Is there anything in particular that would make me choose this tour over, say, the one that picks up down the street over there?"

The lady shrugged. "We've got a big lobster."

She could see that Gabby and I weren't going to purchase tickets. She pulled a phone out of her shirt pocket and looked at the screen through half-lidded eyes, dismissing us.

"But in terms of history, for example," Gabby continued. "Do you get into the history of the city?"

"Excuse us," I said, and pulled Gabby away.

"What are you doing?" I hissed. "This is not helping any-thing!"

"It might have," Gabby insisted. "I was heading somewhere." She let me lead her away from the lady.

"What about walking tours?" she asked. "Maybe our focus is too narrow here. How about those boat tours that take people around the harbor?"

"I don't know," I said. "I think if it was anyone running tours, it would be someone else with a bus. Unless it's not that at all." I let my voice trail off mysteriously, hinting, but Gabby shook her head.

"It must be. Unless it was just a random prank."

"That's what my dad thinks. Maybe he's right."

We walked down the street, heading back in the direction of the library.

Gabby pointed to a sign. "Look. There's one. Portland Land and Sea Tours. Maybe they didn't like your dad competing with the land part of their tour."

"Maybe," I said.

"We should go check it out!" Gabby said.

The sun was in my eyes, and I was starting to feel hungry. It was an uphill walk back to the library.

"I don't think we need to do that," I said. "Besides, I'm not even really sure it was another tour company that vandalized the bus. I kind of have another theory—an idea about someone who might have done it."

Gabby stopped walking and turned to face me. A man walking a dog bumped into her and mumbled an apology. We scooted to the edge of the sidewalk so people could get around us.

"Why didn't you say anything?" Gabby demanded. "Who is it? It's that sweet potato lady you told me about, isn't it? She's unstable."

"No," I said. "It's not her."

"Your upstairs neighbors? The ones who make their cat use a leash?"

I shook my head.

"I thought, maybe . . ."

I pressed my lips together, hesitating. It was very possible I was wrong about Nola, and even if I wasn't, I had no proof at the moment. As hard as it was to believe, Gabby seemed to like her. Maybe this wasn't the time to say anything.

"I just mean that someone else might have done it. I don't really know."

I checked my watch.

"Anyway, we'd better get back to the library. We're supposed to be unschooling there."

"There are all kinds of ways to learn," Gabby reminded me.

"I know," I said. "I'm just not sure if this is one of them."

"Look!" said Gabby, pointing.

The Maine Attractions bus rolled by, stuffed with tourists.

Gabby waved, and a couple of the passengers waved back. The giant fake lobster grinned crazily from the roof as it passed, and I knew we'd been on the wrong trail: anyone could see that this lobster didn't have the brains for a life of crime.

Chapter 7

Unschool Trip

"Mom is in shock," Zenith told me happily a few weeks later.

She had gotten her way about the summer math class, and she and Mom had just come back from signing her up.

"I have a real textbook and everything. I'll be going to school!" she said.

"It's just one class," I reminded her. "And it's just for the summer. And you might not even like it."

"Yes, I will," Zenith assured me.

I didn't pay much attention to her. June had finally arrived after a long, cold spring, and I was feeling good. Dad had a steady trickle of customers riding the tour bus. With no new signs of the vandal, I was focusing on other projects. The school-going world may have been thinking about summer vacation, but Zenith and I were busy.

We often unschooled at the beach, where I plucked crabs from tide pools and examined them while Zenith read beneath a floppy hat. We signed up for swimming lessons (these were exempt from Mom's general avoidance of organized education) at a nearby pool. On rainy days, we went to the library or museums. I had started collecting facts about Portland's history. We kept journals—Mom's idea, though she quickly pointed out that it was a suggestion, not a direction. In addition to history facts, I also liked to write down what I had found while exploring the ocean's edge during the day.

At night, I examined the darkened sky and recorded which stars and constellations I'd seen. Sometimes I made up poems about them. Gabby was with us often, when she wasn't occupied with art club and her modern dance group.

The part I was looking forward to most about summer was that Nola wouldn't be around for a little while. It turned out that every year she went to sleepaway camp for a couple of weeks in June. Gabby told me in a whisper one day that this caused a small yearly rift between Nola's mother and Spirit. Nola's mother felt that camp was completely different from school. Spirit declared that whether you called them counselors or teachers, they were adults determining the best way for children to spend their time.

I didn't care how Nola spent her time, as long as she wasn't vandalizing our bus, and I didn't have to see her.

Zenith flopped down on the couch and flipped through her math book. She began scribbling problems in a notebook, even though her class hadn't started yet.

"Why don't you put that away in our room?" I suggested. "Gabby and Spirit will be here any minute."

Dad's first few weeks giving tours had gone well, so today he had finally agreed to take Zenith, Gabby, and me along on the bus. This would give Mom time alone with one of her life-coaching clients. She had a few of them now.

Zenith turned another page in her book, studied it a while, and applied her pencil to her notebook.

"Zenith? They'll be here soon."

Zenith looked up.

"Why don't you admit that you're scared of what Spirit will say about me going to school?"

"I'm not scared. It's just—if you know someone doesn't like something, why wave it in their face? You don't like mushrooms on your pizza; I don't wave my mushroom pizza in your face."

"Yes, you do," Zenith said matter-of-factly.

It was true. Bad example. I liked watching her squinch up her mouth and pull away from the mushrooms. If it wasn't for Zenith's reaction, I probably wouldn't like mushrooms all that much myself.

When the doorbell rang, I gave Zenith one last glare before turning to answer it. Luckily, it was just Gabby in the doorway. Spirit waved from her car and pulled away.

Mom came into the room, herding us toward the door.

"Okay, girls. We need to leave now if I'm going to make it back here for my three o'clock."

"Is it the sweet potato lady?" I asked. "Or the guy who looks like an onion?"

"Azalea, please," Mom said.

She dropped us downtown, right near Dad's pickup spot. We stood by his sign, waiting. Lots of people walked by, but no one stopped and got in line. I wondered if Dad should have someone to sell tickets on the sidewalk, like the lobster tour bus did. Maybe he couldn't afford to hire someone for that, though.

"There he is," called Zenith.

Dad's bus pulled up to the curb. I barely recognized it. The last time I'd seen it had been the day we painted it in the garage. Now, with the sun hitting it and the bustle of the summer season all around, it looked bright and clean. It looked successful.

A line of people filed off the bus, most of them stopping to slip a bill or two into the tip box next to Dad's seat. My heart beat quickly. This was going to work. Dad was going to hold on to this business.

Gabby danced in place beside me.

"It looks great!" she said excitedly. "I can't wait to take the tour!"

I elbowed Zenith. "He's making it work," I told her.

The tourists who had been on the bus stood on the sidewalk looking slightly dazed. They all seemed to be wearing white sneakers and very new clothing. Some of them had fanny packs around their waists.

"I never doubted he would make it work," Zenith said, much to my glad surprise. Then she finished her sentence: ". . . in the summer. The question is, what's going to happen the rest of the year?"

I put my hands on my hips, refusing to let Zenith ruin my good mood.

"He'll figure out something. And Mom has her clients. This time we're going to stay."

"If you say so."

Our dad raised a palm to us from the empty bus.

"All aboard!" he shouted.

We climbed up and sat in the seat behind him. Inside, the bus looked more familiar. I recognized the red paint above the seats and tried not to think about the angry words hidden beneath it. It had been a one-time prank, I told myself. No one was trying to make us leave.

Other than Zenith, Gabby, Dad, and me, the bus was empty.

"So where are the other passengers?" Zenith asked.

Dad checked his watch.

"I have fifteen minutes before I leave again. They'll start coming on board soon."

We waited in silence for a few minutes, the three of us squished into one seat. Just when it started to seem silly to share a seat on an empty bus, passengers began climbing on. Each one paid Dad, then found a seat. Some of them smiled at the three of us, wondering, probably, why three girls were on the bus without an adult. Gabby and I smiled back.

Most of the passengers were older people, although there was a young family with three small children all dressed in matching red polo shirts.

Dad checked his watch again, and then the sidewalk. There was no one else lined up for the tour. The bus was about half full. Dad pulled the bus door closed and cleared his throat. He leaned toward his microphone, which was mounted on the dashboard of the bus. His tour notes were taped down next to it, written out in large type with the names of streets highlighted. I wondered if he knew the notes by heart yet.

"Welcome to beautiful Portland, Maine," Dad said.

The words drifted weakly back to us. Then he turned on the microphone and said it again. This time his voice echoed through the bus. Some of the people said hello back to him.

"Right now we are in the historic Old Port district of the city, riding along Commercial Street. To your left, notice the US Custom House building, which was completed in 1872."

The tourists turned dutifully to their left, and some held up their phones to take pictures out the bus window. Dad maneuvered the vehicle through the heavy downtown traffic.

"Soon, we'll head out of the Old Port and up historic Munjoy Hill, where we'll get a stunning view of Casco Bay."

Dad pulled the bus up to an intersection.

"Oh, no," he said into the microphone.

There appeared to be the remains of a minor crash up ahead. Two cars sat at strange angles in the middle of the intersection, and several people stood around talking into their phones. No one looked particularly panicked, but two police cars were there, lights whirling, giving an air of emergency.

The road was blocked, so Dad turned left instead of making the right he'd planned.

"So, we're just going to take a little detour, here," he explained to the passengers. He sounded nervous. "Now we're, uh, passing some stores."

There was an expectant silence in the bus.

Dad cleared his throat again. "That's a gelato place, over there."

I squinted at his notes. He had nothing for this street. Traffic was thick; we were barely moving. I could see Dad's shoulders hitch upward, a sure sign that he was tense.

"To your right, notice the T-shirt shop, where you can get, umm, T-shirts. Maybe sweatshirts."

Ahead of us, the light turned red. The bus sat.

"Almost certainly sweatshirts."

"Dad," I said in a low voice. "Don't you know anything about this street?"

Dad switched off the microphone.

"I only know what's in the notes that came with the bus. Somehow I failed to anticipate fender benders."

"*What?*"

"Minor car accidents."

Fender benders. Was that going to be this year's late frost? Not on my watch.

"Dad, turn that thing on," I said, pointing to the microphone. After all, I had been collecting historical facts about the city since we'd moved here. I tapped Gabby and Zenith each on the knee. They had spent as much time in libraries and museums as I had.

"Between the three of us," I whispered, "we can do this."

"Totally," said Gabby.

Zenith shrugged.

I stood up and cleared my throat. With one hand on the driver's seat for balance, I leaned toward the microphone. I knew exactly what to say first.

"On your left, please take a look at these beautiful buildings."

My voice traveled fuzzily through the bus. I bent closer to the dashboard.

"Before 1866, the city was built mostly of wood, but it was destroyed by a fire. All of these brick buildings date back to when the city was rebuilt after the fire."

There. A fine, solid historical fact to kick things off. Pleased with myself, I looked at the passengers. They looked back at me, waiting to hear more. One fact wasn't enough for them. That was okay; I had plenty.

There was just one problem: I couldn't remember any of them.

My mind had gone blank. Where was my fact-collecting journal when I needed it? Home, that was where. I tried to picture it, to flip through the pages, but all I could conjure up was a poem I'd written about how life was like the Big Dipper. I widened my eyes at Gabby and Zenith: *help me out here!*

Gabby stood up and moved toward the microphone. I sat back down to give her room.

"Here's an interesting fact," she said.

Her voice sounded smooth and confident, like she gave tours every day.

"Did you know that chewing gum was invented right here in the city of Portland? In the Curtis and Son building, which is right around here, somewhere."

The tourists looked out the windows helpfully, as though they were trying to locate it.

"It was made from the sap of spruce trees. The gum, not the building."

She sat back down. The three of us had read about this together one day at the library, and then spent an afternoon trying to locate a dripping spruce tree.

The traffic light up ahead turned green and we inched toward it in a line of cars. Dad's shoulders relaxed a little. Before we could get through the light, it went red again. The bus sat. Gabby, Zenith, and I exchanged a panicked look.

This time Zenith came to the rescue, squeezing in front of me so that she could talk into the microphone.

"The Curtis and Son Company," she announced, "started out making all of their gum by hand."

Several of the tourists nodded like they were listening, but a few of them were busy tapping away on their phones. The children in the matching shirts craned their necks to get a look at the tiny screen in their father's hand. *Pay attention*, I wanted to snap. *My sister is speaking.*

"Then," Zenith continued, "the son invented a gum-making machine."

Now that she said this, I remembered reading it. I was glad her memory was so good. We needed to fill as much time as we could.

"In the time it took a worker to make forty boxes of gum the old way," Zenith went on, "he could make eighteen hundred boxes with the machine."

A warning thought flashed through me.

"Zenith, no!" I hissed.

There was no stopping her.

"The question is," Zenith asked the tourists, "how many times faster was the machine than the workers? No calculators! Put those phones down!"

She smiled serenely at the baffled tourists.

"It's summer vacation," the father of the matching kids said. They must have been visiting from out of town. I knew that there were some places where the school year had already ended. "No math for anyone until fall."

Gabby opened her mouth to start explaining about unschooling, but Zenith interrupted.

"Forty-five," she announced. "You just divide."

She sat back down, looking satisfied.

A couple of the tourists clapped politely, as though she had done a trick, and Zenith took a tiny bow from her seat. I shot her a look. Was she *trying* to ruin this tour? But no—she thought she'd contributed quite nicely. Judging by the pleased look on Gabby's face, she thought so, too.

By now, Dad had gotten through the intersection and was steering the bus around a corner. In another minute he was back to the intersection where we had departed from the route. Surely by now the accident would be cleared up and Dad could take over the tour.

Except that the street was still blocked off. Once again, Dad turned the bus the other way. His notes were useless.

And we were fresh out of ideas. The only sounds in the bus were from the traffic outside, and from a game the kids were now playing on their father's phone. An electronic chicken squawk echoed through the bus.

This was a disaster. Dad's business, once again, was a disaster.

"There's got to be more we can say," I whispered fiercely to Gabby and Zenith. "Think! We know so much stuff!"

"I could talk about modern dance," Gabby suggested.

"I could do more math problems," Zenith volunteered.

I put my hands over my eyes and shook my head.

They didn't get it, either of them. Or maybe Zenith did, and she just didn't care. This wasn't just one bad tour. This was everything starting to crumble. This was how it went with Dad. One misstep led to another. The stream of customers would thin. Dad's enthusiasm would wane. He would start casting around for new ideas.

The passengers were beginning to look a little annoyed, and I couldn't blame them. They had paid for a tour of the city, and here we were, sitting in traffic, in total silence. I pushed my way to the microphone again. I took a breath.

"Here we have . . ." I struggled to gather a thought together. Then I remembered some pictures I'd seen, a passage I'd read.

"There's this island right near the city that used to have an amusement park on it. A long time ago. People would go during the summer. It was famous. Back then."

The tourists looked out their windows, searching in vain for the island and the long-ago amusement park.

This was no good. I needed facts about where we were right now, about places people could see out the bus window. Only I couldn't think of anything like that. I would just have to make something up.

"Here we have the site of the former New England Switchel Factory, founded in 1868."

Gabby looked at me with bright-eyed interest: something new to learn! Zenith, on the other hand, knew immediately what I was up to.

Dad kept the bus moving.

"At the time," I went on desperately, "it was one of the country's leading producers of switchel. Which is a kind of drink. Or was. No one drinks it anymore."

Zenith pushed me aside with one hand. I saw a glint in her eye that I didn't like.

"The reason no one drinks it anymore," she explained cheerfully, "is that in the year 1872, the Curtis and Son Company decided to introduce a line of switchel-flavored gum."

"No," I mumbled, burying my face in my hands.

"The new flavor was an instant success. Everyone loved the taste of—"

"Vinegar, molasses, and ginger," Gabby supplied.

"Vinegar, molasses, and ginger," Zenith repeated into the microphone. "Sadly, demand for the gum was so great, the company used up the city's entire supply of switchel!"

I unburied my face to assess the damage.

Gabby looked confused. Zenith looked triumphant. The tourists looked mildly entertained. Dad's shoulders looked two inches higher than they had been at the start of the tour.

"Which is why," Zenith continued, "the New England Switchel Factory eventually sold the building to the Intrepid Society of Unschool Adventurers, which is proud to bring you today's tour."

As though she'd planned it—*had she?*—she ended just as Dad looped again to the street with the accident. The street was clear, finally, and Dad headed the bus toward his planned route.

He cleared his throat and announced, "I think I can take it from here. Over on your right, you'll see Casco Bay."

"What was that?" I whispered to Zenith. "Are you trying to get us in trouble?"

"You started it," she pointed out. "It was just for fun, any-way. We were just having a little unschool on the bus."

"An unschool bus!" Gabby and I said together, and as we laughed I tried not to notice Dad's shoulders, up around his ears, as he conducted the rest of the tour.

Chapter 8

Unschool Board

That evening, Dad peeled potatoes in silence while Zenith and I sliced vegetables for salad. Gabby's mother had picked us all up after the tour was over and dropped Zenith and me back at home. The two of us had been hiding out in our room for most of the afternoon, reading, while Mom met with a client.

I waited for Dad or Zenith to be the first to say something about the tour. I pretended to need all of my concentration to work a sliver of peel from an avocado slice.

Mom entered the room in a burst of cheerful energy, grabbing her apron and flinging cabinets open. The session with her client must have been a success.

"So, how did the tour go? Did everyone have fun?" she asked.

I slid a glance over to Dad, who said nothing. I couldn't read his face. He tossed a potato into a pan of ice water to keep it from turning brown. Zenith sculpted a tomato into perfect sections.

"It went well," I said. My voice sounded high and fake.

I began work on another section of avocado. It was too ripe. I licked some of the mush from my fingers and waited for someone else to say something, but no one did. I tried to catch Zenith's eye, but she would not be diverted from her tomato.

"There was a traffic accident blocking things up, but other than that, it went well," I continued.

"Pepper?" Mom asked Dad. He nodded, and she pulled the pepper mill from the cabinet.

A flicker of a smile played across Zenith's face.

"Azalea," she said, looking down at her cutting board, "I'm thirsty. Would you grab me some switchel from the fridge? Oh, wait . . . I forgot. There's none left, since the New England Switchel Factory has gone out of business."

I couldn't help it; I laughed.

"What's so funny?" Mom asked.

"Apparently, my livelihood is," Dad replied, setting down his peeler. "It's all one big joke to them."

Now Zenith and I were quiet again. Mom waited, trying to understand what was going on.

"We were just trying to help, Dad," I said. "I'm sorry it got out of hand."

"Is this the point of all this child-led education?"

He pronounced *education* in an exaggerated, ironic way, like he didn't think it was education at all. He wasn't even addressing us; he was talking to Mom.

"Children mock their parents and other adults, making things up, thinking that whatever they do is adorable?"

"Of course not," Mom said sternly. "That's not the point at all. What's this all about?"

Zenith sighed and put her knife down in front of a pile of tomato wedges.

"Dad didn't bother to learn anything else about the city other than the notes that came with the bus," she said, "so we tried to help him out when he had to drive down a different street. We *did* help him out. But then we got a little silly, that's all. We didn't mean anything by it."

"We're sorry," I added again.

"Didn't bother to learn?"

Dad's voice had risen. I wasn't used to hearing him yell, and I didn't like it.

"How would you have the slightest idea what I have and have not bothered to learn? Do you think I just got behind the wheel of that bus with no preparation whatsoever? Just because I didn't happen to have dozens of facts at hand when a fluke accident changed my route doesn't mean I take this job lightly. I'll thank you not to make a joke of it in front of the people riding the bus. In case you don't realize it, we're depending on those people to pay our bills."

Say you're sorry, I willed Zenith. *Just say it. You don't even have to mean it. Just say it.*

"I'm sorry," Zenith muttered. She turned to Mom. "How was your session with your client?"

Mom stood frozen a moment, her hand on the pepper mill, debating whether to answer Zenith's question or lecture us.

"It went very well, thank you." Mom's lips formed a slight smile. "The client said I was tremendously helpful."

"Not, apparently, a trait inherited by your children," Dad muttered.

We finished preparing the meal in silence.

It was a relief to all of us that Zenith and I were spending the next afternoon at Gabby's. When Mom dropped us off, Gabby was waiting on her front lawn. She hugged us both, then led us around to the backyard, where we sat on the steps in a patch of sunlight. Gibran and Charlie were in front of the shed, their tarp spread out and littered with wood. If they'd made any progress since the last time I'd been there, I couldn't see it.

"Is this the famous boat?" Zenith asked, walking right over.

Gabby and I remained on the steps, watching.

"It's gonna be," mumbled Gibran. "We hope."

Zenith studied the blueprint, still spread out on the tarp. It was a little crinkly where I had spilled the switchel, but otherwise it was fine. Zenith nodded at the boards.

"So these are the sides."

"Yeah," Charlie said. "But they came out wrong."

Zenith knelt down for a closer look at the plan.

"What are these sets of numbers—like here: one, eight, two?"

"That's how you know where to mark your wood," Gibran said. "That's feet, inches, eighths of an inch." He tapped one of the boards with a pencil. "We put a nail in at each of the marks and bend a thin piece of wood around them to give us the curve of the side."

Zenith nodded. She wasn't acting silly around Gibran, like I'd thought she would. She was genuinely interested in the boat. The ones who had acted silly, I realized, were Nola and Gabby and me. Mostly me.

"Here's the trouble," Charlie said. He showed Zenith the piece of wood he'd asked Nola to hold up the day I'd been there. "See how it doesn't fit flush against the sides?"

"Looks like you measured the angles wrong," said Zenith. She peered at the blueprint again.

"Yeah," Gibran agreed. "We need to redo it."

86

"Hand me your protractor," Zenith said. "Maybe you can just recut the one angle instead of starting the whole side over."

Gabby and I ambled over to the tarp to watch. If Nola had been with us instead of Zenith, we probably would have resumed our annoying little sister routine. Zenith wasn't like that, though. I knew I didn't want to be like Nola. But I was surprised to find that I wanted, at least right now, to be like Zenith.

"I think I found the mistake," Zenith said.

She was on her knees on the tarp, comparing her measurement to the number on the plan. "Take a look."

The boys gathered closer to see, and Gabby leaned over Zenith's shoulder. I waited for Zenith to swat her away, the way she would do to me if I got that close, but she didn't.

"Here," she said to all of us. "See how the angle is too wide? It just needs to be cut again."

"We'll need the jigsaw," Gibran said, picking up the board.

We all followed him to the woodworking shed.

"You guys can come in," he called over his shoulder. When he met my eye, his mouth formed a lazy smile. "As long as you don't plan to spill anything in here."

I flushed for a second, remembering the soaked blueprint, and then I smiled back.

Zenith's head tilted the tiniest bit; she was curious. I had told her about the time we'd made switchel, but I'd left out the part about knocking the glass over. I hoped she had seen Gibran smile at me, without hearing what he'd said about spilling. I wanted Zenith, just for a moment, to wish she could be more like me.

At the end of June, Nola made her triumphant return from camp. She showed up at Gabby's one afternoon when Zenith and I were over there.

The three of us were part of the boat project now, just as naturally as if it had been the plan all along. Zenith had taken to the whole thing immediately: the blueprint, the tools, the measurements. And her enthusiasm had swept Gabby and me in, as well. We learned how to slice the end of a board with a block plane and how to mix epoxy, a strong glue. We learned that fiberglass is a kind of cloth, not a kind of glass.

And now Nola had come to spoil it all.

I spotted her first. We had all been crammed inside the shed, which was wired with electricity and housed an astonishing variety of woodworking tools. I stepped out to grab some sandpaper that I'd left on the tarp, and there she was, her sunburned skin as pink as her dress.

"Where's Gabby?" she called to me, not bothering to say hello.

I jerked my thumb toward the shed, and Nola's jaw dropped.

"She's in *there*? Do the boys know?"

I shut my eyes to try to keep her voice from piercing into my brain, but it didn't work.

Nola flounced past me and flung herself inside the shed.

"What's going on in here? Did everyone miss me?"

"Nola!" I heard Gabby say. She sounded glad, but I thought I detected just the tiniest bit of flatness in her voice. I stayed out for another second or two, enjoying the Nola-free air, and then went back into the shed.

"No way!" Nola was shouting, looking at the boat, which by now really looked like a boat. We were getting ready to put the seats in.

"I can't believe you did all this without me! I know so much about boats from camp!"

"Dial it back, Nola," said Charlie.

Nola gave him a dirty look.

"Come on," she said to Gabby, and, by extension, to me. "Let's go in the house. This is boring."

This time, it was me who ignored Nola, not the other way around. I slid on a pair of safety glasses and began sanding the edge of the board that was to be one of the seats.

"Come *on*," Nola said impatiently to Gabby. "I want to show you videos of my camp friends."

"Actually," Gabby said, picking up another pair of safety glasses, "I'm kind of busy in here. Maybe we could do that later."

She glanced at me and I smiled.

Nola sighed heavily and sat on a pile of boards. Of course she wouldn't leave by herself; she needed an audience. But no one listened as she chattered away. We were hard at work, and when Gibran carefully slid a piece of wood through the power jigsaw, the fierce noise of the metal blades silenced her. I had never seen such a useful tool in all my life.

That evening at dinner, Dad seemed to be in a good mood. He smiled at Zenith and me when we came to the table and asked us about our day.

"It was okay," Zenith said. "We're working on a boat."

"You mean, like, a job? Will you be at sea for many months?"

"Like, a project," Zenith clarified. "At Gabby's house."

"Aha," said Dad.

"I told you about the boat," I reminded him. "You know this already."

Mom ladled corn chowder into bowls and passed them around while Dad sawed a loaf of bread into slices. I reached for the salad tongs and loaded my plate.

"Nola's back," I announced. "Her weeks at Annoying Camp have really paid off."

"Here's something funny," Dad said, resting his spoon in his bowl, leaning the handle against the edge. I watched to see if it would slip down under his soup.

"Tell us," said Mom.

"I was just on the phone with my old friend Robert." Dad looked at Mom. "You met him once, I think, back in Philadelphia." Mom nodded.

"Well, get this," Dad said. "You know what he's doing now?" He paused for effect. "Llama farming!"

He bounced the sides of his hands comically against the table, and his spoon slid right under the surface of the chowder and disappeared.

I glanced at Zenith to see if she'd noticed, but she was looking down at her own bowl, stirring and not eating.

"In Philadelphia?" asked Mom.

"Texas," Dad told her triumphantly. "Isn't that something? The guy's got a hundred acres of land and he's raising llamas, of all things. He sells their hair. People use it to make sweaters."

"Why would you need a llama-hair sweater in Texas?" I asked. "Isn't it hot there?"

"It's never too hot for a downy-soft, top-quality garment composed of one hundred percent genu-wine llama hair!" Dad said in his game-show voice.

Then he got more serious.

"It's not just their hair that makes them valuable. People use them to guard other animals, and carry packs up mountains, and all sorts of things."

"Sounds like a strange enterprise to me," Mom commented. She pushed her empty bowl aside and started on her salad.

"Well, there must be a market for it, because apparently old Robert is cleaning up."

"I'm sure he is," Mom said, forking a chunk of tomato, "what with all those llamas on his land."

I snorted and looked again at Zenith, who was pretending not to hear.

"You're a riot," Dad said. He looked at the table for his spoon, then at the floor. Then he stood up in some confusion to go get a new one.

Later that night, in our room, Zenith was extra sulky. She sat on her bed, her math textbook open, scratching out problems in her notebook.

I couldn't figure her out. Just a few hours ago, at Gabby's house, she'd been having a great time. We'd come home and had a nice family dinner. Then, *wham!*, Zenith was in a foul mood.

"That's my pencil," I told her.

I was sitting on my own bed in my pajamas, watching her.

"See those hearts on it? That's mine. Gabby gave it to me. She has all these pencils with stuff on them."

Zenith threw the pencil across the room at me without even looking up. It could have hit my eye. She would have been in a lot of trouble, if that had happened. Instead it hit the wall and fell down on my bed.

"What did you do that for?" I yelled.

Zenith slammed her books onto the little table by her bed.

"You just don't get it, do you, Azalea? You're just so happy with your little projects and your new best friend and your perfect life, you don't even see what's right in front of your face."

I felt cold all of a sudden. I'd thought I was pretty good at seeing what was in front of my face.

"What on earth are you talking about?"

"Llamas." Zenith spit the word out with a mix of loathing and triumph.

"You mean, Dad's story about the guy he knows? What has that got to do with anything?"

Zenith glared at me.

"Llamas, Azalea. Think about it. Do you remember, by any chance, a day in North Carolina, when we owned the breakfast place, when Dad told a funny little story about a guy he knew who owned an apple orchard in Connecticut? And do you remember a day in Connecticut when Dad told a funny little story about a guy he knew who drove a tour bus in Maine? Do you follow me?"

"That's stupid, Zenith. You're making a big deal out of nothing."

I hugged my knees to my chest. But I did remember. Now I remembered exactly.

Maybe it didn't mean anything this time. Maybe sometimes a story was just a story, not an ominous hint that our lives were about to change. After all, things had been going great. Or, at least, pretty well. Mom had clients; Dad had passengers.

"Fine. Have it your way," Zenith said.

She switched off her light, got into bed, and faced the wall.
She probably hadn't even brushed her teeth. Good. If I was going

to end up an eyeless victim of pencil attacks, she could end up toothless.

I opened the bedroom door and went out into the hallway to say good night to Mom and Dad. I could hear them talking in the kitchen, so I headed that way. I mostly didn't mean to sneak up and listen, but something made me stop before I went in.

Mom was talking; I could hear from the rhythm of her voice that she was reciting a list.

"I'm getting more clients; you're giving tours like you planned; the girls are doing well. Can't we just try to make this work?"

"Don't you think I *want* to make it work? What do you think I'm out there doing every day? I'm on a razor-thin profit margin here, and if I don't see some better numbers in July and August, I can't see how this business is going to keep us afloat."

I heard Mom's impatient sigh.

"And you think Texas is the answer?"

"I'm not saying it's the answer. I'm saying it sounds like a viable option if this turns out to be a mistake."

Texas, then. Zenith had been right.

My mother's voice rose a little.

"And I'm saying that I don't think we should be looking at another move right now. Not to mention the fact that I imagine llamas are more difficult to raise than apples, and we didn't do so well with the orchard, did we?"

"That's completely different, as I'm sure you're well aware. Llamas, for starters, can survive a frost."

"How on earth do *you* know what llamas can survive? Since when are you an expert on llamas?"

I gave up on saying good night and crept back to the bedroom.

Zenith had put the light back on and was sitting cross-legged on her bed. She had opened her math textbook and notebook again. She had retrieved my pencil, also known as her assault weapon, and was working it busily on the paper.

I got in bed and turned my face into the pillow so Zenith wouldn't see my tears.

I needn't have worried. She was absorbed in her books, taking fierce enjoyment in figuring out the answers to the sort of problems that could be solved.

Chapter 9

Unschool Break

A couple of days after the llama fight, the bus vandal struck again.

The day had started out well.

I'd been working on something for Dad. I presented it to him right after breakfast, as he was getting ready to leave for work.

"Look," I said, handing him a sheet of paper. "It's for you."

Dad looked at the paper. Zenith pretended not to care what it was, but I saw her pause on her way to our room.

"What's this?" Dad asked. He read from the paper. "Ten Things You Didn't Know About Portland. One: the first telephone system in the city was installed in 1878. One of the phones was in the office of a coal supply company. The other was in the company's coal storage area."

He looked up from the paper, amused. "The first phone system in Portland consisted of two telephones connected to each other?"

"That's right," I said. "And the place where that coal company office used to be is right next to your pickup spot. Now it's that restaurant with the deck that overlooks a parking lot instead of the water. You could point it out right when you start the tour."

Dad looked down and kept reading.

"Two: Lincoln Park was created after the fire of 1866. The area used to have a lot of wooden buildings, but they burned in the fire. City workers decided that having a rectangle of open space in the city would help keep another fire from sweeping through."

"You pass right by that little park on your tour," I explained. I pointed at the paper. "You also go right near the Abyssinian Meeting House, which is believed to have been a stop on the Underground Railroad. You should talk about that."

"Azalea!" Mom said, reading over Dad's shoulder. "This is wonderful! Thank you."

Zenith quit pretending to ignore us and joined the conversation.

"Where did you get all of this stuff?"

"Oh, I don't know. Library. Museums. Books. I thought since I was collecting it anyway, I might as well give Dad a list. Something for the tour."

Dad looked grateful and embarrassed both.

"Thank you, Azalea. This will be very useful, I'm sure."

"You're welcome," I said.

I hoped Zenith was properly jealous of me and how helpful I was. If she was, she hid it well.

"I'm going to keep this right up front with my notes," Dad said. He folded the paper carefully and slid it into his shirt pocket. Then he headed for the front door.

"Have a good day!" Mom called after him.

"Bye!" I yelled. The door shut, and Dad was gone.

We did not have swimming that day, so Zenith and I had a lazy morning ahead of us until she had to be at school.

Zenith packed her bag with her math book, notebook, and pencils. I drew planets on a sheet of paper. I had studied the existing planets with Mom, back when I homeschooled. I decided that as an unschooler, I would invent a few of my own. I looked through my box of colored pencils and selected an orange one.

Then, about a half an hour after Dad had left, he was back. He stalked into the living room.

"What is it?" Mom asked, looking up from her journal.

I had a feeling that she was still writing down how Zenith and I spent our time, a habit from homeschool days. Yesterday's entry probably said: *Zenith created an educational adventure by exploring the urban environment on her bicycle. Azalea got glue everywhere.* (I'd been trying to build a toothpick aquarium. For a while, before I tried adding the water, it had seemed like a really excellent idea.)

"There are nails sticking out of the tire," Dad said.

I didn't understand at first. I thought he was talking about the car.

"What do you mean?" asked Mom. "The bus rolled over a nail and now it's stuck in the tire?"

The *bus.* Of course.

"No," said Dad. "I mean, someone took a hammer and pounded half a dozen nails into the right front tire of the vehicle. It wasn't an accident. Someone put them there very deliberately."

Mom rested her forehead against the palm of her hand.

"Why is this happening?" she asked.

Zenith and I just stood there. I was holding my breath, and had to remind myself to breathe.

"I don't know," Dad said.

"Call the police," Mom insisted. "This needs to be addressed. Call the police."

"What are the police going to do?" Dad asked wearily. "I don't think they're going to assign a special task force to ferret out a tire nailer."

"Maybe they could find some clues," I said helpfully. In books I had read, bad guys always left clues, and usually children found them and solved the mystery.

"There were no clues," Dad assured me. "People don't leave fingerprints on tires, and even if they did, no one is going to waste time on something like that."

"You're certainly determined to make sure nothing gets done about this," Mom said grimly.

"Are you making this my fault?" Dad asked.

Zenith cleared her throat. "It's time for my class."

Mom grabbed the car keys, but she didn't move. Instead, she asked Dad, "Now what?"

"Now I wait until three o'clock, which is the earliest I could get a service person to come to the garage and replace the tire. And I miss a day's work."

I had a feeling that this wasn't what Mom meant. She was probably thinking about those llamas in Texas. I knew I was, and it was a pretty safe bet that Zenith was, too. But we all acted like she was talking about the repair.

As the three of us headed out the door, I turned toward Dad. I felt sad that no one was saying good-bye to him. "See you later," I said, but he didn't seem to hear.

In the car, no one spoke. Some tiny thought picked away at me, trying to make itself heard, and then finally it spoke up in my mind, loud and clear.

Nola.

The whole time Nola had been away, nothing bad had happened to the bus. Now she was back from camp, and there were nails sticking out of one of its tires.

It all made sense.

Nola must hate me more than ever now. Since she'd been back, she'd hung around on the edges of the boat project, complaining and trying to get Gabby to do something else. If she spoke to me at all, it was to whine about the noise from the tools, or the smell from the epoxy, or whatever else was bothering her. She hadn't ever been interested in working on the boat, it turned out; she just liked to be at the center of whatever was going on. And she liked to order Gabby around. If Zenith and I moved away, she would have Gabby all to herself again.

After Mom dropped Zenith at school, she let me off downtown in front of Basil's Grab Bag, a store that had a little bit of everything, though not necessarily what you needed at any given time. Gabby and I were meeting there to do some shopping while Mom did errands.

"I'll be back in half an hour, Azalea," Mom reminded me for the hundredth time as she pulled over to the curb in front of the store. "Please be waiting outside for me."

"Okay, Mom," I said.

Spirit's car pulled up behind us, and Gabby sprang out onto the sidewalk. I got out of our car and the two of us hurried inside.

"I have a list of stuff I need," Gabby said. "Do you think they have string here? I need a lot of it. Also, some new flip-flops."

But I had more pressing business. I grabbed Gabby's shoulder as we walked past a display of beach balls and sand chairs.

"You'll never guess what happened."

"What?"

"It's the bus again. The unschool bus. Someone put nails in one of the tires."

Gabby whirled to face me. "No!"

"Yes. Someone is determined to force us out of Maine."

I wasn't quite ready to say Nola's name. Meanwhile, I liked the way my voice sounded, kind of quivery and frightened.

"It sounds like it," Gabby agreed. She stared into the distance, eyes narrowed, like a detective in a movie. I wondered if this was the time to mention Nola. Then Gabby pointed toward an aisle that was labeled HARDWARE.

"We need to look there," she announced.

"For string? Or flip-flops?"

"Neither. We need to look at nails. We need to learn everything we can about them, and then we'll go to the bus and see what kind of nails the vandal put in it, and we'll figure out what kind of person would use them."

"You mean, like, based on personality?"

An exasperated look flickered across Gabby's face; for the briefest second she reminded me of Zenith.

"No. Based on job. Or hobby. Are they nails a carpenter would use? Are they the kind of nails you would use to make something small, like a box for tips, if you were a competing tour company?"

I couldn't take it any longer. "Or the kind you would use to build a boat?"

"What?"

"What if the vandal is someone we know? Someone who has access to nails because of the boatbuilding project."

Gabby looked bewildered. "Who on earth are you talking about?"

I waited until a customer finished selecting a box of sandpaper and moved into a different aisle.

"Gabby, haven't you noticed how much Nola hates me? And it was her uncle who owned the bus. Maybe he left his keys behind when he moved, and she took them. Maybe she's doing all this so my family will have to move away."

I hadn't even told Gabby about the llamas yet. Just thinking about them made me want to cry.

Gabby laughed. "Come on. Seriously. Who do you think is doing this?"

I paused. I stirred my finger through a bin of bolts.

"I think it's Nola. Nothing bad happened the whole time she was at camp, and she comes back to town, and boom! There are nails in the unschool bus tire. And you know perfectly well that she can't stand having me around. You know it's true."

"Azalea!" Gabby cried. Her eyes filled. "I know you and Nola haven't exactly hit it off, but that doesn't mean you can go around accusing her of crimes!"

I looked at the floor.

"I didn't accuse her. I'm just saying that I think a lot of the evidence points to her."

It seemed like a phrase Gabby would use.

"What evidence?"

"I already told you. She obviously doesn't like me. Maybe she never wanted her uncle to move away. Maybe she doesn't like that my family took over his bus."

The more I said it, the more possible it seemed.

But Gabby was shaking her head slowly.

"And the timing," I continued. "You have to admit, it looks pretty bad for her."

"I can't believe you'd think that. I can't believe you are standing here telling me you actually think that Nola vandalized your family's bus. Twice."

"I didn't say I was sure," I said quickly. "I just said it seemed like a possibility."

"Well, don't say it again," said Gabby.

I followed her in silence around the store as she collected and then paid for her items. We left the air-conditioned cool of the building to wait on the sidewalk for our mothers. Everything looked shimmery in the heat, and the buildings did not seem familiar. I felt as if I were lost and alone in an unknown city.

Spirit's car arrived first, and Gabby hurried over to open the door. She didn't look back at me, or wave. She left without saying a word.

I laid low for the next few days, avoiding any mention of Gabby at home so no one would know we'd had a fight. The last thing I felt like doing was talking about it. I didn't need to hear my whole family saying what a dumb idea it had been to tell someone that you suspected her good friend of being a bus wrecker. I already knew.

Luckily we were pretty busy, so no one noticed that I hadn't seen or spoken to Gabby. After we had swimming in the morning, Mom took Zenith and me shopping for desks, which she said we ought to have in our room. If Zenith was going to spend half her time solving math problems, Mom said, she should be able to sit up straight while she did it. I didn't feel like I needed a desk, but if Zenith was getting one, I wanted one, too.

Mom dragged us through half a dozen dusty secondhand stores, looking for two desks that sort of matched. This project took two afternoons, and it kept Zenith interested enough that she didn't mention going to Gabby's to work on the boat. Then it was the Fourth of July, which turned out to be Dad's busiest day of the season. He barely had time for a break, so Mom, Zenith, and I met him at his stop with lunch and snacks. That evening, we all went to watch fireworks. We spread a blanket on the small patch of grass we'd staked out on the hill overlooking the bay. It seemed like the whole city was out there. I wondered if Gabby was somewhere in the crowd.

I was finishing lunch a day or two later when Mom walked into the kitchen, waving her phone.

"That was Spirit," she said. "Good news! She's invited us to a party she's giving this weekend. A midsummer celebration."

"Like a late Fourth of July party? Or a solstice party?" I asked. "Even though both those things already happened?"

I tried to sound casual, unalarmed. I wondered if Gabby had told Spirit about what happened. Was Spirit mad at me, too? Was a midsummer celebration really a say-good-riddance-to-friends-you-no-longer-like party?

"It's not for solstice or Fourth of July. Spirit says it's a celebration of the full moon and friendship and all the energies being aligned." Mom waved her hand vaguely. "You know Spirit. Anyway, it'll be nice."

She didn't give any sign that she knew about my argument with Gabby.

"Is it, like, a good-bye party?" asked Zenith, reading my mind. "Like, a nice-to-have-known-you-for-a-short-time-before-you-move-on-to-your-next-place party?"

"No one's moving on to a next place right now," my mother said sharply. "What makes you think that?"

"Logic," said Zenith. "The same set of conditions will always lead to the same outcome. It's just a question of when."

Mom drew a breath to begin arguing with Zenith, but I interrupted.

"I don't know if I feel like going to a party," I mumbled.

Mom put a hand on my forehead. "Don't you feel well?" she asked, her face full of concern.

"I don't know. Maybe I'm getting sick."

Mom touched her lips to my face expertly.

"You don't have a fever." She narrowed her eyes at me. "Is there something wrong?"

"No. I'm just going to go lie down."

I went into the bedroom and shut the door.

A few minutes later, Zenith came in.

"What's this about, Azalea?"

"Nothing. And I could ask you the same thing. What was that about with Mom, and the logical outcome?"

"You know exactly what I meant. There was never any chance we were going to last here. We'll be lucky if we even get to see the boat finished."

I had been lying on top of my bed. Now I pulled the quilt over myself up to my chin. "It's almost done. We just have to paint it."

Except that I wouldn't be painting any boat. Not with Gabby not speaking to me. It looked like Nola had finally gotten what she wanted: Gabby, all to herself.

"I'm sure there will be plenty of llama barns for us to paint in the near future," Zenith said. She paused. "So what is it, anyway? What's wrong?"

"Nothing."

"Yes, it's something," said Zenith. "You've been moping around for, like, two days. And you haven't been talking about Gabby. Did you have a fight?"

"No," I said, but my voice got thick and my face crumpled.

"You told her that idea of yours about Nola, didn't you?" Zenith asked. But her voice wasn't mean and knowing. It was kind, and a little sad.

"Yeah."

"Listen," said Zenith. "Don't say that to her again. Just drop it."

I nodded.

"And don't get all upset. Fights happen. Mom and Dad fight. You and I fight. But it doesn't last forever, right?"

"Right," I said, wiping my nose with my wrist.

Zenith made a face and handed me a tissue from a box on her dresser.

"So this one won't, either. I bet you'll patch it up right away at the party."

"Thanks," I told Zenith. "I hope you're right."

"I'm on a streak," she said.

Chapter 10

Unschool Reunion

Spirit had told her guests to come at around eight-thirty, so we could all be together when darkness fell and the full moon made her glorious appearance in the sky.

After dinner, Zenith dressed carefully, pulling on a skirt and running a brush through her thick, straight hair. I ran a brush over mine, too, being careful not to get the bristles in too deep, so they didn't get caught in the tangles.

I didn't feel like getting dressed up. I didn't even feel like going. I wondered if Gabby would talk to me. Even worse—I wondered if she had told Nola what I'd said. I imagined the two of them, huddled together, whispering about me, following me with glaring, angry eyes when I walked past. I almost hoped that Zenith was right—that we would move again soon.

Except that wasn't what I wanted at all.

Dad drove us all to Gabby's, with Mom directing. He had never been there before.

It took us a while to find a place to park on the street, because there were so many cars. Spirit must have invited a lot of people over. We had to walk to their house from a ways down the street, and when I pointed out the house to Dad, his eyebrows lifted.

"Wow," he said. He turned to Mom. "I see what you mean."

"About what?" I asked.

"Nothing," he said.

"He means that Spirit has a lot of money," Zenith told me.

I thought about this.

Rich people, as far as I knew, had servants and long, fancy cars, and ate food off silver trays with covers that the servants removed. Spirit, Gabby, and Gibran didn't live that way. On the other hand, I'd never heard anything about Spirit having a job, and they did have that large house filled with beautiful things, and that silent car. Was this another way to be rich—a sort of secret way? And how did Zenith know?

I wondered what else everyone knew that I didn't.

The front door was open, and we could hear voices and laughter from inside. Normally I went in through the back door, but there seemed to be some kind of party rule in place. We entered the house and wove through the crowd, looking for Spirit. I looked around for Gabby but didn't see her. Maybe she was purposely avoiding me, watching me from some distant corner, sharing jokes and secrets with Nola.

We made our way to the kitchen, where Spirit was ladling out mugs full of soup. It reminded me of the unschool meeting, when I'd first met Gabby.

Paper moon cutouts hung all around the food table. I tried to find potato chips, but Spirit only served chips made from loftier vegetables. I selected a pinkish one that might have been a radish once. I stuck one end of it into a bowl of bean dip and ate it quickly so I wouldn't have to taste it. I wondered if Gabby had made any cookies, and I felt a sadness slip into my throat.

And then Gabby was standing there, greeting us even before Spirit had seen us.

"Welcome!" she said, but it seemed more like she was talking to my family as a whole, not to me in particular. "Happy Midsummer!"

"Happy Midsummer!" we all said.

"Aha! It's the boatbuilders!" Spirit said to Zenith and me, sloshing soup onto the counter.

She turned to my parents. "Learning through doing! What a wonderful way to gain understanding."

I waited for Zenith to say something about how she was gaining understanding at school, too, just to needle Spirit.

"It *is* a great way," Zenith agreed. "I'm learning some really interesting stuff in my math class too, but we don't talk much about how to use it in real life. That's something I think unschoolers do a lot better—apply ideas to real life."

Spirit nodded toward Zenith, smiling.

Zenith smiled back. They seemed to have reached some sort of truce. They might even have been on their way toward becoming great friends.

Maybe if we moved to Texas, I could find a nice llama to be my friend.

"The kids are all outside," Gabby announced. "Come on."

I couldn't tell if she was talking just to Zenith, or to me, too.

We followed her through the kitchen door to the backyard.

The sun was very low, and the mosquitoes were out. Spirit had put citronella candles around the deck to discourage them, but it didn't do any good. The air was growing cool. I had on a short-sleeved T-shirt, and I shivered a little, slapping at my arm where something had bitten me. At least I was wearing jeans. Zenith must have been freezing in her thin skirt.

I could see Gibran and Charlie across the lawn. The boat was in front of the shed, upside down on two wooden sawhorses.

They were on their hands and knees in the damp grass, studying it from beneath.

Zenith headed right over to join them. A few other kids I didn't recognize darted around. Someone rocked back and forth in the tire swing, and in the distance I could hear Nola's shrieky laugh.

Gabby and I stood side by side, looking across the lawn at the boat. Someone raced by, calling out to her, and Gabby lifted a hand in response. We stood there a while longer.

I spoke first.

"I shouldn't have said anything. It was stupid of me to say that about Nola. I didn't mean to make you upset. I'm really sorry, Gabby."

I felt Gabby's hand on my shoulder.

"I'm sorry I got so mad," she said. "It's just that . . . I know Nola can be annoying. I know you don't like her. But she's not a bad person. I don't think she would do something like that."

"I know," I said.

But I didn't know. I felt like I didn't know much of anything.

"The thing is," Gabby went on, "I've known Nola forever. Our families are really close, and we do unschooling stuff together and everything. It's like she's related to me. I didn't exactly pick her, but she's there."

"She sure lets you know she's there," I said.

"I know." Gabby dropped her hand and turned to me. "Azalea, the thing is, I need both of you. Nola is like my cousin or something, but you're my best friend. And it's really hard for me if the two of you don't get along."

I felt tears come to my eyes. *We were still best friends. Gabby was still my friend.*

"I understand what you're saying," I said. "I'll try harder to like Nola—or at least to get along with her."

Gabby smiled. "Thanks."

We stood in silence for a minute.

Gabby looked across the lawn. "Looks like Zenith is hard at work."

Zenith had bent down to look underneath the boat with the boys. She crouched on the grass next to them, carefully holding her skirt against the back of her legs.

"She's worried that her *home*derwear is going to show," I said.

And then Spirit was outside, leading a brigade of adult guests, clapping her hands together.

"Everyone, everyone!" she shouted. "Can we gather in a circle? It's almost that time!"

"Here it comes," said Gabby.

"Here what comes? What's it almost time for?" I asked.

"You'll see."

Zenith and the boys came over from the boat. Someone bounced across the yard and flung an arm around Gabby. Nola. It was hard to see color in the failing light, but I was almost sure she was wearing pink.

Everyone arranged themselves into a ring. *Lucky the yard is so big*, I thought. I saw my parents across the circle, and though I couldn't make out the expression on Dad's face, I could imagine it. It was the same look he'd had when he asked my mother if she was going to be paid in root vegetables.

Spirit stepped into the middle of the circle and raised her arms to the sky. She tipped her face upward and her long hair fell back. Her loose-fitting dress billowed and swung around her.

I glanced up at the sky to see what she was looking at. It wasn't the best night for stargazing. Some clouds hung low, and there was a glow where they obscured the moon.

Spirit lowered her gaze to the circle of guests and began to speak with what I was beginning to recognize as her leading-the-people voice.

"Hello, friends," she intoned. "Those of you who have celebrated the midsummer full moon with us before are aware of a certain tradition we have."

A low wave of laughter spread across the yard. Whatever the tradition was, it was apparently pretty funny.

"And for those of you who are new to our celebration, I welcome you and urge you to join in without reservation."

She paused, allowing suspense to build, and I waited for her to deliver the big news.

"We gather on this midsummer's evening beneath the light and the healing power of the moon. I encourage you all to feel her energy. I encourage you all to let the healing energy in, and let the negative energy go. Let out the sorrows and the disappointments of the past. Acknowledge them, and then let them go. Send them flying off into the universe without judgment. They are the past."

Then Spirit tipped her head back again, so that it faced the dark sky. She took a deep breath and let out an enormous, eerie howl, a long, clear, strange sound that sliced through the dark.

"Now, everyone," she commanded, "howl!"

The sound multiplied as Spirit's guests joined in.

I hesitated. I had never howled before.

I looked at my family, and none of them were howling. Nola's fists were clenched and her throat was working; she must have been waiting all year to let loose.

Next to me, Gabby nudged me with her elbow.

"Come on, try it. It feels good."

She turned her own face toward the cloudy blotch of moon-light and let out a surprisingly loud howl.

I joined her.

"Howwwoooooo," I yelled, and it *did* feel good. I wasn't sure if I'd ever made that loud a noise before, even yelling at Zenith. I howled again, and a third time. I could barely hear myself over the noise everyone was making, but I could feel the rawness in my throat, the exhilaration of hurtling sound out into the night.

I looked over at Zenith; she was howling. So was Mom. Dad was looking at the ground. Either he'd finished howling, or he didn't plan to start.

And then it was done. Spirit held her arms up for a moment of silence, and then she turned silently and walked back inside the house. Most of the people followed her.

"There's cake in there," Gabby explained to me.

Still, we didn't go inside. We stood in the yard, which was dark now, and cold.

"The boys and Zenith forgot to cover the boat," Gabby said. "And it's supposed to rain tomorrow."

We walked to the corner of the yard and each of us grabbed a corner of the tarp that lay crumpled on the grass. We yanked it up over the boat.

"Not that water should hurt a boat," Gabby pointed out. "But we'll need it to be dry when we paint it. Maybe in a couple of days, if it isn't raining."

She bent down and picked something up.

"I keep finding stuff out here that belongs in the shed," she told me. I could see that something was glinting in her hand. "The other day it was an extension cord, sitting right out in the grass." She bent to the ground again. "Here's another. Nails. All over the yard."

Our eyes met and then we looked away from one another. Neither of us wanted to think about that day at the store. I helped Gabby collect the nails from the cool grass and we put them on top of the tarp.

"Azalea?" Gabby asked when we were done. "Is it true that you might move away?"

I jammed my hands into my pockets. It was really chilly, now that the sun had set all the way.

116

"Who told you that?" *Was it Nola?* I almost asked. But I stopped myself.

"Gibran said that Zenith mentioned it, one day when you guys were over here working on the boat. He just told me about it this morning. He said Zenith told him you were probably moving to Texas."

I didn't say anything.

"It's not true, is it?"

There was silence.

"Zenith thinks it's true," I admitted, finally. "But Mom says no one is going anywhere right now."

"Why does Zenith think it's true?" Gabby's voice sounded strained.

"Oh, she has this idea. She says it's logic. She says the same conditions lead to the same outcome. Meaning, that if you keep doing things the same way, they'll always end the same way. Like, Dad tries a new business and it doesn't make any money, and then he gets a new idea about something else he can try, and we move again."

Saying all this depressed me. I had been trying to forget about it.

"And is this just like those other times?" asked Gabby.

"Not for me, it isn't," I said. "I never made such a great friend before."

Gabby put her arm around me and gave me a squeeze.

"And it's different for Mom, too," I continued. "She's got her own work now. She's got clients, and she's getting more of them. So that's different. That's a reason to stay."

I began to feel a little better.

"What about Zenith?"

I thought a minute.

"I don't know. She definitely likes working on the boat. She likes her math class. And you heard what she said to Spirit inside. She likes doing unschooling stuff along with taking her class. I think she's pretty happy, for Zenith."

"She must be pretty *un*happy, though," Gabby pointed out, "if she likes it here but she's convinced you're moving again."

"She *is* convinced of that," I agreed. "She even said we probably wouldn't get to see the boat painted."

"No!" Gabby cried. "But we're going to do that really soon!"

"I know! It's like, not only is she totally sure we're moving, she thinks it's going to happen any second now!"

"Maybe she wants it to be like ripping off a Band-Aid," Gabby said thoughtfully.

"What do you mean?"

"Maybe she thinks that the faster it happens, the less it will hurt. Maybe that's why she's talking about leaving so soon."

I turned this over in my mind. "Maybe so."

The back door to the house flew open, throwing a triangle of light onto the deck, and a familiar figure loped toward us.

"Gabs! There you are! Aren't you coming in for cake?"

"In a second, Nole," Gabby called.

I hoped that would send Nola back inside, but no; she had honed in on Gabby and was heading our way. Nothing would stop her until she'd yanked Gabby away from me and pulled her across the yard.

In the seconds before she reached us, Gabby spoke to me in a quick whisper. "You don't still think Nola did it, do you, Azalea?"

"No," I told her, because at that very moment, just before Nola wrapped her hand around Gabby's arm and began piloting her toward the house, I finally saw everything clearly.

I understood exactly who had vandalized the bus.

Chapter 11

Unschool Work

"I have to find my family," I told Gabby, pushing past her and Nola. "I have to get inside."

I ran into the house, where people were eating slices of cake off small, fragile plates.

I found my parents and Zenith standing near the food table.

"Can we go?" I asked.

Mom took a close look at my face. "Are you okay, Azalea?"

I wasn't; I felt sick to my stomach.

"I'm just tired," I said. "I'm ready to go home."

Everyone was starting to leave, anyway. Apparently after the howling and the cake, the party was finished. First, though, Mom had to locate Spirit, and then wait her turn in a tangle of guests to thank her for having us over. Spirit had to hug each one of us, and then she called Gabby over to tell us good-bye, and then there was another round of hugging.

It took a long time for us to reach our car, and when we did, we rode home in silence.

I waited until Zenith and I were in our bedroom with the door shut, and then I let her have it.

"I know it was you," I said, shaking a little. Every nerve in me felt alive, hot with anger.

"What was me?" she asked, half-listening, rummaging through her bureau for her night things.

"The bus," I said.

Zenith turned around.

"What are you talking about?"

She folded her arms across her chest and looked at me scornfully, but I wasn't fooled. I understood now. It all made sense.

"You did it. You took Dad's keys and rode your bike to the garage. You probably stole his map showing how to get there when you stole the keys."

My voice sounded different, louder and sharper than normal.

"You bought the red spray paint and wrote those words, and later you took a hammer and nails from Gabby's house and hammered the nails into the bus tire."

Zenith tried to keep the scornful look in her eyes, but I knew her too well. I could see the layers of fear and sadness underneath.

"And why would I have done that?" she asked.

"Because," I said, my voice rising, "you never wanted to come here. You never believed that Dad could make this work. All you wanted was to see him fail, so you could say 'I told you so' to everyone, and talk about how every one of his businesses fails, and go around in a terrible mood and make everyone feel bad and be better than everyone with your math and your know-it-all-ness and your going to school and not being a real part of the family!"

"That's not true!" Zenith said. She was crying now; I had made her cry, and it felt good. She deserved to cry.

"I did not want to go around saying he failed. I just knew that he would. Because yes, he always fails. He starts something and he doesn't finish it, and then we all have to move and he tries something else and something goes wrong and we have to leave."

Zenith blotted her nose with a tissue and took a shuddering breath before continuing.

"You saw the tour he gave that day we were on the bus. He didn't know anything. He had no idea what to say when he had to take a different street. It never occurred to him to try to learn anything other than what was on those original tour notes. And your writing those facts for him wasn't going to change things. Nothing is going to change who he is."

I watched Zenith. I forced myself to speak calmly. I would not cry. This was Zenith's time to cry, not mine.

"So what was your plan, Zenith? What did you think would happen? We would go back to Connecticut and the orchard would be waiting for us and we'd never have to move again? Or we'd go to Texas and somehow that would be better than being here?"

"I didn't have a plan," Zenith whispered. "I just figured that if he was going to make a mess of this and move us somewhere else, it might as well happen sooner rather than later. Before we got settled in here and it got harder to leave."

"That's idiotic," I said. "That makes no sense."

But I understood it completely. It was exactly what Gabby had said about the Band-Aid. Furthermore, it was probably true. It *would* hurt less the sooner it happened. It would have hurt a lot less if I'd never met Gabby—but what did Zenith care about that?

The anger surged up in me again.

"What about me?" I demanded. "How incredibly selfish was it for you to try to ruin things between Gabby and me?"

"I had nothing to do with your fight with Gabby. You're the one who stupidly told her you thought it was Nola."

"Don't call me stupid!" I screamed. "And I'm not talking about that—I'm talking about never seeing her again if we move away! You're going to make us have to move away!"

The tears I'd been holding back streamed down, and then our door flew open and Mom and Dad were in the room with us.

"What is this?" Mom asked. "What's going on?"

"Tell them," I shouted, mopping tears off my face with my wrist.

Mom and Dad stared at us. Zenith looked back at them, defiant and ashamed. For several seconds, no one moved. Then Zenith spoke.

"I'm the one who did the stuff to the bus."

Mom and Dad said nothing. I saw Mom's face twist into disbelief. Dad's jaw set. We all stood and waited. The sudden quiet made my ears ring. It seemed like we stood there for a long time, not moving.

"And why did you do that?" Dad asked finally, his voice low and level. "Why did you frighten your family and cost me hundreds of dollars in repairs and lost time? Do you have a reason?"

Zenith said nothing. She tilted her head slightly—a nod.

"And do you want to tell me that reason?"

Mom laid a hand on Dad's arm.

"Maybe we should discuss this tomorrow," she said shakily, "when everyone is calmer."

"I'm perfectly calm," Dad said, "and we will discuss it now. Zenith, why did you misbehave in such a spectacular way?"

I had begun to shiver a little. I sat down on my bed and Mom sat next to me, putting her arm around me.

"Because I figured we were going to end up leaving here anyway, so I thought I'd just speed up the process."

"And why did you think we were going to end up leaving here?"

"Because we always do," mumbled Zenith.

Then she grew bolder.

"No matter what I did to the bus, things were going to end the same way. You can't make a year-round living doing seasonal bus tours. And I heard you talking about Texas, anyway."

"I was talking about Texas," said Dad slowly, each word an icy shard, "because someone was sabotaging my tour business."

"That's not true!" I shouted.

Suddenly, I was angry with Dad, not Zenith.

"There was only the one time with the spray-painting, right at the beginning. Then everything was going fine. You were talking about the llamas *before* the thing with the tires happened. Zenith is right! You move us from place to place and try job after job, and we never get to stay *anywhere*!"

Zenith nodded in agreement.

How had we gotten to be on the same side?

Dad looked from Zenith to me.

"I'm just trying to do what's best for the family. That's all I've ever . . ."

His voice caught. He cleared his throat as though he planned to continue, but he didn't. He sat on the corner of Zenith's desk and looked down at his hands.

Now Mom spoke. "Zenith, are you unhappy here?"

Zenith was crying again.

"No," she said. "Not really. At first I was, I guess, but now I like my class, and going to the beach, and doing stuff with Azalea and Gabby."

Had I heard right? Zenith liked doing stuff with me?

"I like doing stuff with you, too," I sniffed.

"And I am too a real part of the family," Zenith shot at me.
Mom got up from my bed and went over to her.

"Of course you are," she said, hugging her. "Who said you're
not?"

"Azalea," she said in a muffled voice, up against Mom.

"Well," I said defensively, "she's always in a bad mood about something. And she doesn't even really unschool, because she goes to school some of the time."

"That has nothing to do with whether she's a real part of the family," said Mom. "We're a family because we love each other, not because we never get in bad moods or because we unschool."

I imagined her saying something like this to the sweet potato lady, something firm and kind and impossible to argue with. She was probably an excellent life coach.

"I think," said Dad, "that we need to do some negotiating."

Everyone looked at him. He stood with his arms folded, his face tense.

"First, we all need a promise from Zenith that nothing like this will ever happen again."

"It won't," she said softly. She looked around at all of us. "I'm sorry."

"I know you are," Dad said. "I am, too. I'm sorry you've been unhappy about moving, and I'm sorry that you chose this way to communicate your unhappiness."

"What's the rest of the negotiation?" I asked.

We had dwelt on Zenith's mistakes long enough. It was Dad's turn to offer something.

Dad sat heavily on Zenith's bed. We waited for him to speak.

"The rest of the negotiation is, first, me saying that *I'm* sorry. I'm sorry we've moved around a lot. I'm sorry things haven't always worked out."

Haven't *ever* worked out, I could hear Zenith thinking.

"I've always tried to do what's best for all of us. All the different moves we've made, they've been for our family—so we can have the best possible life."

"We know that," Mom said, but Zenith and I said nothing.

"I guess it's been for me, too, though," Dad went on. "I guess some part of all that moving has been selfish. I wanted to have my own business, not work for someone else. I wanted to chart my own course." He smiled a little. "Like an unschooler."

"We can understand that," Zenith told him.

"Yeah," I agreed. "I guess that makes sense."

Dad nodded. "And I can understand how you all want to stay here."

"All?" I asked.

"That's right," Mom said. "I want us to stay here, too. Dad and I have been discussing this for a while now. He and I have not entirely seen eye to eye."

"I'm rethinking my position," Dad said, "and I think it's pretty clear that we have a consensus. Everyone wants to stay."

Mom still had an arm around Zenith.

"You're sure?" she asked Dad. "I want us *all* to be sure."

"I am now," Dad told us.

I didn't dare look at Zenith. I didn't move. I didn't want to undo the moment.

"I know we can make it work here," Mom said, her voice full of energy. "I'm getting more clients. That'll help us through the off-season."

"And I'm going to find a job for the winter," Dad said to Mom, "like we talked about. Then I'll start running tours again in the spring."

"Then you'll still have your own business, even if you work for someone else sometimes," said Zenith. "Just like I still unschool even if I take a class sometimes."

Dad smiled. "I guess that's true. I hadn't thought of that."

Then his smile faded, and his voice grew stern again.

"We still need to talk about your actions, Zenith. You cost us a lot of money, and frightened everyone."

"I know," Zenith said softly.

"You're going to work off your debt by helping me. That means taking tickets for me before tours, cleaning the bus, whatever needs to be done."

"Okay."

"Okay, then."

We sat for a while longer, but no one had anything else to say. We all said good night, and Mom and Dad left the room.

Zenith and I got into our beds. I lay in the dark for a long time, listening to Zenith breathe. Although I was exhausted, it was hours before I slept.

The next morning was quiet. A steady rain fell, so Zenith and I couldn't go swimming. It would be a bad day for tours, but Dad went out anyway.

I wanted to chatter to Mom and Zenith about how we were going to stay here—about how we didn't have to move away ever again, maybe—but they didn't seem to be in the mood for it. They were each holding their thoughts to themselves.

Partway through the morning, the doorbell rang. I sprang up before Zenith could, and opened it.

It was Gabby and Spirit.

"Gabby!" I shouted. She was exactly the person I wanted to see. Wait until she heard what Dad had said about us not moving. And wait until she heard about Zenith and the bus! So much had happened since we'd seen each other the night before.

But Spirit was standing right behind Gabby, looking like they were there for a purpose.

By this time, Mom had come into the room. "Hello!" she said, sounding surprised. "Come on in! We had such a good time at your party last night."

I could see that she was trying to compose her face, to look like everything was normal.

"Wasn't it cleansing?" Spirit asked. "We can't stay—we're on our way to Gabby's art club—but we wanted to drop this by. You left it at the house last night."

She handed Mom a sweater.

"I didn't even realize I'd left it behind! Thank you," Mom said. "Are you sure you don't want to come in and have some coffee?"

Gabby and I looked at each other hopefully, but Spirit shook her head. She didn't turn to leave, though. She studied all of our faces.

"Something is different here today. The energy. What's wrong?"

"Nothing," Zenith said quickly from behind a book. She was settled into a chair in the corner.

Gabby and I looked at each other again, and her eyes opened wide, questioning. I widened mine back: *you'll never believe it.*

"It's the bus, isn't it?" Spirit demanded. "Gabby told me about how someone put nails in one of the tires and whatnot. Did it happen again?"

"No," Mom said, looking at the floor. "We've resolved that."

"It was me," Zenith said then.

We all jumped a little.

She laid her book on the table next to her and stood up. She fixed her gaze on Spirit.

"I did a stupid thing and I'm really sorry, and it's over now."

"Oh, Zenith," said Gabby sadly. She looked at me, her chin trembling, and then back at Zenith. "Don't you like the unschool bus?"

"It's okay," said Zenith. "I guess I do."

"Why on earth would you have done such a thing?" Spirit asked.

Zenith paused a moment. I saw a thought play across her face, a sort of dare she was giving herself.

"It was kind of a math thing," she said.

Spirit drew herself sharply upward; this was what came of attending school!

"I mean," Zenith continued, "that I was sort of experimenting with an equation. I thought I knew what all the pieces would equal; I thought the outcome was already set. But I was wrong."

No one said anything for several seconds. Gabby looked like she was going to cry. Mom put her hands on her hips, as though she planned to take control of the situation, but she remained silent.

Then Spirit leaned forward and laid a palm against Zenith's cheek.

"There are all kinds of ways to learn a lesson," she said.

Chapter 12

Unschool Cheer

I didn't know which was more surprising—that the boat was ready, or that Mom and Dad were letting Zenith and me take part in its inaugural sail.

Of course, they had crammed us into life vests, and we weren't actually venturing into the ocean. That had been strictly forbidden. Instead, the boat was to be launched in a pond a little ways from Gabby's house.

August was drawing to a close, and the early-morning air had a bite to it. We had agreed to launch the boat early, so Dad could be there before he started work for the day. This late in the season, he said, every tour, every passenger, every dollar counted. There would be another wave of tourists in the fall, the September and October leaf-peepers, but then that would be it for the year.

Dad had already lined up his job for the off-season: he was going to cook in a health-food restaurant. When tour season came back around, he hoped to keep working there part-time. Mom had taken on three more clients. The sweet potato lady, it turned out, had a lot of friends.

We drove to the pond, and when we pulled into the small parking lot, we could see that Gabby's family was already there. So were Nola and Charlie and their mother. Otherwise, the pond was deserted. A damp fog hung over the water. I was glad I'd

worn jeans and a sweatshirt, and I didn't even mind the life vest. It was an extra layer.

Zenith and I ran down to the edge of the pond, where Gibran and Charlie had the boat sitting on the wet silt. They were both barefoot, with their pants rolled up, discussing how best to push the boat off into the shallow water. Gabby and Nola stood next to them.

"The water's too shallow," Nola pointed out.

I was glad to see that everyone else had life vests on, too, not just Zenith and me. Nola's was orange, and I bet she was annoyed about that.

"It's going to just sit on the bottom when we all get in," Nola added.

"Then maybe we won't all get in," Charlie said.

I liked the idea of leaving Nola on the shore, but I knew he was just joking.

"It'll be fine," Gibran said. "We just have to wade out a little deeper. She's right that it's too shallow here."

Nola glowed with pride. Then she saw Zenith and me. "Zale! Zenith! You're here!"

"Hey, Nola," I said.

We hadn't exactly become friends, but almost. I knew Gabby would never tell her that I'd thought she was the unschool bus vandal. I still felt kind of guilty about it; Nola wasn't that bad, once you got used to her. She wasn't that great, either, but I was learning to live with her.

Farther up the beach, Mom and Dad stood with Spirit and Nola's mother. Mom waved, and I waved back.

"Azalea, get your shoes off," Zenith ordered, pulling off her own.

I kicked off my sandals and rolled up my jeans.

"Are we ready?" asked Gibran.

"Ready," we all answered.

The boys pushed the boat off the muddy bottom of the pond so that it floated on top of a foot or so of greenish, weed-clogged water. All of us cheered, including the parents. The boat had passed the first test—it floated.

I had to admit, it looked good. We had painted it white, with its name in dark blue letters: *The Unschooner*. That was Zenith's idea; she'd had to explain to me that a schooner was a type of sailboat.

Bugs skittered over the water's surface, and I tried not to think about them as I set a foot in the pond. I yelped a little; the water would warm up later in the day from the sunshine, but now it was an icy shock to my skin. Gabby and Nola yelped, too, as they waded in, but Zenith acted like all she ever did was start the morning bare-legged in a cold, dank pond.

"I guess Gibran's better at unschooling than I thought," admitted Gabby. "I can't believe we actually built a boat that works."

"It floats," corrected Nola. "We'll see if it can hold people."

"Not just any people," I added, sliding a glance at Gabby. "The Intrepid Society of Unschool Adventurers."

Gabby laughed, shivering a little.

The boys pulled the boat deeper and then motioned for Gabby to climb in. She hesitated for a moment; the water was at least waist-deep for her, but she bravely waded out, soaking her shorts. Then she grabbed on to the side of the boat and struggled a little. I remembered her trying to do skin the cat at the park. Gibran grabbed her waist and heaved her up into the boat. It rocked crazily, and Gabby screamed, but with delight in her voice.

"Just sit still," Charlie told her.

She settled into the seat at the front of the boat.

He turned to me. "You, next."

I grabbed the side of the boat, and it rocked toward me.

"Careful!" said Charlie. He hoisted me over the side and I slid next to Gabby on the seat.

Next came Nola, her pink sweatpants pushed up as far as they could go. Gabby and I each grabbed one of her hands and pulled her in. She jammed herself in between us on the seat.

Zenith, Gibran, and Charlie stood in the water.

"Who's going to row?" asked Zenith.

"We can take turns," said Charlie. "You want to go first?"

"I'd like that."

She pulled herself up into the boat and settled herself facing backward in the rear seat: rowing position. Then Charlie climbed in and crouched down on the floor—already wet from our feet—in the middle of the boat, between the two seats.

"Here we go," said Gibran.

He grabbed the back of the boat and shoved it farther out into the pond. His T-shirt ballooned around him in the water beneath his life vest. He heaved himself up into the boat and plunked himself down next to Charlie. The boat pitched for a minute or two, and I held my breath. Then we leveled, and Zenith slid the oars beneath the surface of the pond.

From the shore, the grown-ups cheered, and all of us waved to them except for Zenith, who was busy rowing. Sunlight filtered through the damp air. A bullfrog belched. No one, not even Nola, spoke. We listened to the slap of the oars against the pond.

In a little while, we would switch rowers, and the boat would respond wildly to the shifting weight. I would grip the side of the boat with one hand, and Nola's arm with the other, watching the cold sludge at our feet roll back and forth. When the rocking settled, Nola would ask crankily where we were headed, and Gabby would remind her that the journey itself was the important part.

This would all happen a few minutes later, when the sun was slightly higher in the sky. For now, we sat quietly. We glided over the water. The boat held steady.